WILL
AND THE MOTORWAY HORSES

BARRY LILLIE

Flatfield F

Copyright © Barry Lillie 2020
Cover design by Flatfield

The moral right of Barry Lillie to be identified as the author of this work has been asserted in accordance with the Copyright, Designs and Patents Act of 1988.

All rights reserved. No part of this publication may be reproduced, stored in a retrieval system, or transmitted in any form or by any means, electronic, mechanical, photocopying, recording, or otherwise, without the prior permission of the copyright owner of this book.

This novel is entirely a work of fiction. The names, characters and incidents portrayed within are the product of the author's imagination. Any resemblance to actual people living or dead is entirely coincidental.

You can follow Barry on the following platforms:
www.barrylillie.com
www.facebook.com/barrylillieauthor
www.instagram.com/barrylillie2
www.twitter.com/barrylillie1

For news about new releases and free content sign up for Barry's Book Club here:
barry@barrylillie.com

For

The Renegade Writers
with grateful thanks for their sound advice,
unwavering support
and of course, for laughing in the right places.

Chapter One: The New Human

Chapter Two: Chocolate Eggs

Chapter Three: The Silver Box

Chapter Four: Cheese

Chapter Five: Joshua-James

Chapter Six: Lady Godiva

Chapter Seven: Visitors

Chapter Eight: A Good Idea

Chapter Nine: Pantomime

Chapter Ten: The Last Mince Pie

Chapter Eleven: Happy New Year

Chapter Twelve: Willow's Surprise

Chapter One: The New Human

The stable door opened and the day began like every other. Chestnut, the old Shire-horses in the corner of the stall; conker coloured and standing eighteen hands, with a fine white blaze on his forehead and creamy feathered hooves, yawned. He flicked his mane and farted as the other horses woke up: You could say he was an equine alarm clock.

The sand-coloured pony named Willow stood up, stretched her legs, and shook her mane before trotting out of the stable into the weak February sunshine, making her way, as she did most mornings, down to the fence at the bottom of the field.

The fence overlooked the long grey path, that the humans called the M6. Willow watched as boxes on wheels raced past each other; some flashed their eyes angrily, while others made a hooting noise to show their displeasure.

Willow often stood gazing out over the fence; she liked to look at the deep indentation in the grey path, that the horses called the bumpy hole.

The bumpy hole had just appeared one morning in the motorway, and the humans that sat inside their boxes on wheels tried to avoid it. Those who didn't navigate around it properly found they'd thump into and out of the hole, much to the little pony's pleasure.

Willow also shared her home with Applejack, her grey dappled friend, Bramble and Copper, the two fillies and Roger the donkey, and despite the noise from the M6 and the scent of diesel in the air, this happy group of equines enjoyed living together.

As usual that morning, their stable door had been opened by Mr O'Leary, the human who looked after them all. Chestnut had once told the others, that Mr O'Leary had been a traveller who had married a non-traveller and had now settled down to life as a gorger. Willow had asked Chestnut what a gorger was but had been told, that he had no idea, as he was just a fucking horse.

The boxes on wheels had begun to slow down to a crawl, as they did every morning when Willow heard a rumbling sound. She turned around to see a man-human arrive at the gate on a two-wheeled seat. Mr O'Leary walked towards the gate and the two-wheeled seat stopped rumbling. "Follow me, I'll show you the fucking horses," he said. Willow watched as the new human began to climb over the gate. "Don't clamber over the gate like that, use the sodding stile you dimwit," Mr O'Leary shouted. "You'll bugger it."

"Sorry," the man-human said, and then losing his footing as he swung his leg over, he slipped, falling chin first into a pile of yesterday's horse shit.

With quizzical looks on their faces, Applejack and Roger trotted out of the stable, possibly disturbed by the commotion at the top of the field. Willow trotted over and wished them both a good morning. "What's going on, and who is that with Mr O'Leary?" said Applejack.

"I don't know. He arrived a few minutes ago."

"It's Mr Neville, he's Mr O'Leary's nephew," said Roger.

"How do you know that?"

"I heard him telling another human. He said that his good-for-nothing nephew had moved into something called a flat in Bloxwich and that the lazy-arsed bastard was coming to work for him."

"Roger," Willow asked, "what's a nephew?"

"I don't know, because I'm a fucking donkey."

Mr O'Leary made a clicking sound with his mouth, and the three friends' ears pricked up. At the bottom of the field, Chestnut lifted his head from the patch of grass he was eating and Bramble, who could be a vain filly, stopped looking at her reflection in a puddle. Copper, her black ears upright, poked her head outside the stable door and whinnied, "Did someone call?"

"Mr O'Leary. He made the clicking sound," said Willow.

"That means he wants us to go to him."

Copper left the stable and joined the others and together the six friends trotted up the field, splitting into two groups as they circled the big tree that stood in its centre, before regrouping and heading in the direction of the two humans standing at the gate. As they approached, Mr O'Leary said, "Here they are lad, now there's no need to be afraid, they're all quite gentle; but do be careful of the donkey, he bites. The miserable little shit." Willow liked being thought of as gentle and ears facing forward, she smiled. After hearing Roger referred to as a miserable little shit: a thought many of the others also shared, she suppressed a giggle.

Very quickly, the horses became used to Mr Neville's daily routine. Every morning he'd open the stable doors and the horses would leave to watch as he used a door opening stick to unlock the brick box with the square glass eye at the top of the field. Mr O'Leary kept sacks of feed and various other important things inside the brick box with the square glass eye. He'd told Mr Neville, to make sure that he never left the field without securing it.

One of his first jobs was to take out a sack containing food and pour it into the horses' manger. Willow was pleased that Mr Neville never forgot to make sure that the horses also had fresh water and she also enjoyed it when he would bring each of them a fresh apple as a treat: Something Mr O'Leary had never done.

One morning Mr Neville was inside the stable putting down fresh straw, when Applejack brushed against the coat that was draped over the door. As the grey horse's flanks touched the waxy jacket a piece of paper fell from it, fluttering to the floor.

Applejack was looking at the paper when Willow joined him, "What's that?" she said.

"It's fallen out of Mr Neville's jacket. Do you know what it is?"

"It's a piece of paper," said Willow, as she nudged it with her nose, opening it up.

"What are those odd marks on the paper?"

"They are words. The humans use words on paper to communicate with each other."

"Interesting," said Applejack. "What do the words say?"

"I don't know, I can't read the humans' words, because I'm a fucking pony."

Willow looked up to see Chestnut running across the top of the field. "I think we should ask Chestnut, he's such a clever old horse, maybe he'll know?"

"What a splendid idea."

As the old Shire's run slowed to a trot, he snorted and tossed his creamy-coloured mane before walking over to join Willow and Applejack. "What do we have here?"

"Paper and words," said Willow. "We were wondering, as you're the oldest and wisest of the horses if you would know what the words are saying?"

"I doubt it; you see I'm a fucking horse."

"I guess we'll never know," moaned Applejack.

Mr Neville finished replenishing the straw inside the stable and was picking up his coat when he spotted the piece of paper on the ground. He stroked Willow's forehead before bending down to pick it up. "Mustn't lose this, it's important," he said folding it and placing it back inside his coat pocket. "Did you hear that?" said Willow. "He said it was important."

"Yes," said Chestnut, "How intriguing."

The three horses watched as Mr Neville walked up the field, he was a short, squat man who looked a little like a drum with stumpy legs. He had a round and cheerful face that matched his disposition; however, the early onset of male pattern baldness coupled with his girth and his rather languid way of moving gave him an air of clumsiness.

He usually had small white buds that played music inserted into his ears as he went about his chores, and quite often he'd sing random lines from the songs he listened to. A few days earlier Bramble had commented on his singing, saying if she heard him belt out 'Jumpin' Jack Flash' one more time, to shut him up she'd have to bite him in the ass, ass, ass: Bramble pursed her lips as none of her friends understood her song related joke.

This morning Willow saw him open the brick box with the square glass eye; he put the stick with the U-shaped spikes that he used to pick up hay with inside and took out a sack of horse feed. He filled the feed trough and as usual, Copper, the black pony was the first to saunter over and begin eating. Mr Neville was stroking her chunky neck when he took the piece of paper out of his coat pocket and read what was written upon it, before walking over and pinning it to the tree nearest the footpath that ran down past the gate.

"What's Mr Neville fixed to that tree?" Bramble asked, joining her friend for breakfast. "It looks like a letter," said Copper "I heard Willow tell Applejack that humans use them to communicate."

"What do you think the letter says?" Bramble asked.

"I couldn't possibly say," mumbled Copper, through a mouthful of horse nuts. "You see, I'm a fucking horse."

Meanwhile, at the water trough stood Roger; he was also watching Mr Neville, who was now using a finger to stab at the surface of the talking oblong that he kept in his pocket; the talking oblong that also sometimes played a tune to indicate that another human wanted to talk to him.

Now it was well known among the horses that Roger was rather nosey and often listened into conversations that were none of his business, and more than once he had upset one of the others by gossiping about what he'd heard. Today however what he overheard would prove beneficial.

Roger left the water trough and sidled over towards Mr Neville, who now had the talking oblong pressed against the side of his head as he spoke. Pretending to nibble at a patch of nettles, Roger listened and being somewhat of an expert when it came to deciphering one-sided conversations, he heard something that would prove to be very important indeed.

After Mr Neville stopped talking, he put away his talking oblong and climbed onto his noisy two-wheeled seat, and with the back wheel kicking gravel into the air, he sped away.

Roger used Mr Neville's absence to his advantage and strolled over to where Willow and Chestnut were standing, "I know something, you don't know," he said. Because you see, the donkey could often be an irritating little tit full of his own self-importance. "Really?" said Chestnut.

"Yes, it's about the letter that Mr Neville fixed to the tree."

"Do you know what the letter says?" said Willow.

"Yes. Well, sort of."

"Can you read it?" Chestnut asked.

"Of course not, I'm a fucking donkey."

"So how do you know what it says?" said Willow.

"I heard Mr Neville say, that Mr O'Leary no longer wants horses, and because there's no money in them, he wants to replace them with cows in the future."

"Cows?" said Chestnut, his voice booming with disbelief.

"But, what will happen to us?" said Willow.

"Mr Neville said Mr O'Leary has tried unsuccessfully to sell us."

"Sell us, oh dear."

"He said that Mr Clifford the vet would be coming out to put us all to sleep in three days."

"Oh bollocks," said the old Shire.

"We must tell the others right away." Willow began to walk away when Chestnut took charge. "Now there's no need to panic. I suggest we wait until Mr Neville has secured the stable tonight and when he's left for the evening, we can then discuss the situation with the others. Until then, let's try to keep this among ourselves."

That evening, the horses gathered around Chestnut as he told them all about the conversation that Roger had overheard earlier that day. "Are you sure we can believe him?" said Applejack, not able to disguise the suspicion in his voice. "We all know what a troublemaker he can be," said Copper.

"A little shit," said Bramble.

"Piss off," spat Roger.

The three horses and the donkey began to argue and it looked as if things were about to get out of hoof when Willow cleared her throat loudly. "Look everyone, there's no point in us all falling out; we need to come up with a solution to this problem." She stood up, taking position next to Chestnut and said, "I've been giving this some thought all afternoon."

"All afternoon," said Bramble. "You've known about this all afternoon?"

"Yes, but that's not important now, what is important is what we're going to do about it."

"What can we do?" moaned Roger.

"As I said, I've been giving the situation some thought and, well, If Mr O'Leary wants cows, then that's what we'll give him."

"What are you talking about?" said Copper.

"There's some spotted fabric at the back of these old stables."

"So?" sniped Bramble; at times she could be as spiky as her name.

"I can make each of us a cow suit and we could disguise ourselves."

"And how will you do that?" asked Roger.

"There's an old cloth-joining machine in the back room too."

"Can you use one of these machines?" Chestnut enquired.

"Of course she can't," said Bramble. "She's a fucking pony."

"Well actually," said Willow. "Yes, I can."

"Well then," Chestnut said, "I think it's a splendid idea."

So that night Willow set about the task of making the cow suits. She began by cutting out the cloth and then poked the end of the fastening thread through the eye in the pointy thing, that was attached to the cloth-joining machine.

Before long it was bobbing up and down, attaching one piece of fabric to another.

It took Willow two nights of constant work to make the six suits. On the morning of the third day, the horses waited until Mr Neville had gone inside the brick box with the square glass eye and without delay, they put on their disguises before stepping outside the stable into the field.

Moments later, Mr Clifford arrived with Mr O'Leary and they stood at the gate looking bemused, there were no horses to be seen, not even a miserable old donkey. For inside the field stood six magnificent looking cows. "My assistant must have sorted the horses out," said Mr O'Leary. "I'm sorry I seem to have wasted your time."

"I'll still be sending you a bill," Mr Clifford, the vet said. Because you see he was a nasty money-grabbing piece of shit.

***

Weeks passed and the horse-cows continued to fool Mr O'Leary; even Mr Neville, who saw them every day, was taken in by their disguises.

But one day, as the bluebells appeared under the hedges and winter promised to give way to spring, Roger the donkey-cow was to hear Mr Neville speaking into his talking oblong, and again what he heard, caused him to worry.

Chapter Two: Chocolate Eggs

The spring sun was setting and as the evening established itself, an orange glow illuminated the field beside the motorway. Chestnut and Willow stood watching the boxes on wheels as they thundered along the M6. "Dear oh dear," said Chestnut, as a red box flashed its eyes angrily at a silver one; then bellowed with its horrid monotone voice. "These humans, they are always in such a rush, I think that they should relax more."

"I much prefer the mornings when they all slow down, almost to a stop and bunch up. It's much quieter then," said Willow.

"I agree," said Chestnut.

"I wonder why they do that every day; it's almost as if all the humans are trying to get to the same place at the same time."

"That's homo sapiens for you," the old horse-cow told her. "They're an odd species."

Willow turned away from the fence to see Bramble and Copper enjoying an early evening gallop. The two young horse-cows chased after each other, laughing as they ran. "You're too slow," Bramble called over her shoulder to her friend.

"You're too fast for me," said Copper.

"It's because you've put on so much weight lately," laughed Bramble. Who could sometimes, without thinking, say quite unkind things.

But it was true, Copper had always been a bit of a greedy guts, gobbling more than her fair share of hay and oats, and she couldn't walk past a sack of horse nuts without plunging her nose into it and stealing a mouthful.

The two horse-cows stopped running, and panting they trotted over to Applejack, who was standing just inside the doors of the stable. "Good evening girls," he said.

"Evening," they both replied in unison.

"What have you been up to today?"

"Not much," said Copper.

"Just having fun," Bramble said, nodding in Willow's direction.

Willow nodded back and leaving Chestnut to his thoughts, she strolled over to join the others. As she trotted across the middle of the field she spotted Roger standing alone beneath the big tree. "Evening Roger," she called out.

"Yeah, whatever," the grumpy donkey-cow mumbled, before turning his back to her, raising his tail to let out a noticeably loud fart.

"I wonder what's up with Roger," she said as she reached the other horse-cows. "He's just a miserable twat," said Bramble.

"No, I think something is troubling him," said Willow.

"How can you tell?" laughed Copper, "He's always been a moody old sod."

"Haven't you noticed that he's been keeping himself to himself lately?"

"So, no change there then," said Applejack, much to the amusement of Copper, who let out a loud whinny.

"Steady on, Copper," said Willow urgently, as she spotted a fat white, box on wheels arrive at the gate. "Remember you're supposed to be a cow."

"Sorry."

Mr Neville climbed out of the fat white box on wheels and walked around to the other side. "It's Mr Neville, I wonder why he's come in one of those fat white boxes on wheels?" said Applejack.

"I heard Mr O'Leary say that the fat boxes are called, vans," Bramble said matter-of-factly.

The horse-cows watched as Mr Neville opened the side door and a pair of fat black legs followed by a woman-human climbed out. "Looks like Mr Neville has brought Miss Trudy today," said Willow.

"Miss Trudy?" said Applejack.

"She's Mr Neville's lady friend."

Miss Trudy, now free from the fat white box on wheels, leant on the gate and said, "Ooh, they're strange looking cows."

"Cheeky bitch," muttered Bramble.

"She needs to talk," whispered Copper.

"I know, look at her, she's like an over-inflated rugby ball."

"And only half as attractive." Miss Trudy looked away as the two friends snorted with laughter.

Mr Neville clucked his tongue and the horse-cows trotted over to join him. Willow preferred Mr Neville's cluck, it was gentler than the harsh double-click made by Mr O'Leary. Chestnut also began to walk towards the humans, but Willow noticed that Roger remained at the big tree with his back to everyone.

Mr Neville checked the feed trough and then opened up the brick box with the square glass eye. Miss Trudy unloaded cartons from inside the fat white box, and the horse-cows watched as she stacked them by the gate. Willow was pleased to see that even Roger appeared to be interested and began to shuffle his way up the field.

"I've cleared a space for the eggs, just under the window inside the store," said Mr Neville

"Shall I take them straight inside?"

"Yes please, I'll just get the animals settled for the night." He clucked his tongue once more and shook a bucket containing carrots as he walked down the field towards the stable.

Once inside, Mr Neville gave each of the horse-cows a nice fresh carrot before reaching down and feeling between their back legs. This was something he did twice a day and no matter how many times he had a fidget with his digits, they couldn't get used to it. "Nothing there; *again*," he said; the emphasis being upon the word, again. Then shrugging his shoulders, he closed the stable door for the evening and walked away.

"Do you know something," said Bramble. "Things have been quite good since Willow had the idea that we dress up as cows and I've even quite enjoyed fooling the humans. But I just cannot stand it when Mr Neville has a poke around between my legs. Pervert."

"What's a pervert?" asked Copper.

"The dictionary definition says it's a person whose sexual behaviour is regarded as abnormal and, or unacceptable," said Willow.

"Do you know any perverts?"

"No, because I'm a fucking pony."

The horse-cows settled down for the evening. It didn't take long for Chestnut to start snoring, sleep coming quickly to the old Shire. Willow rested her head upon a straw bale and pretended to be asleep, ignoring Copper who had just asked, "What's a dictionary?"

***

The next morning after opening the stable doors and filling the food and water troughs, Mr Neville had left the horse-cows alone in the field. They were all enjoying their breakfast when a loud crunching sound came from over the fence, "What was that?" said Bramble.

"I'm not sure; shall we take a look?" said Chestnut.

With the exception of Copper and Roger, the others galloped down the field to see what had made the noise. Over the fence, the boxes on wheels had come to a standstill and in the middle lane of the M6, smoke rose from the front of a crumpled box that was kissing another one, but at a very odd angle. Instantly the four friends turned their heads to the right as they heard the wailing and flashing lights of two boxes on wheels charging headlong down the narrow path that ran down the left-hand side of the motorway.

***

Even though she had already eaten breakfast, Copper was sniffing around the brick box with the square glass eye, looking for the horse nuts that often got spilt when Mr Neville took out the sacks of feed.

A scraping sound caught her attention, and Copper looked up to see the square glass eye move in the breeze. She lifted her neck and with the side of her nose she tapped the metal frame with a sideways movement, and the glass eye opened.

The young filly looked all about. Noting that the others were too busy watching the incident over the fence to be bothered with what she was doing, she lifted herself onto her hind legs and peered into the brick box. In the corner, she could see the neatly stacked sacks of feed and her mouth began to water. "I wish I could reach in and lift one of those sacks out through the square glass eye," she said. "If only there was something I could stand on; something to make me tall enough to reach inside."

Right beside the open window were the cartons that Miss Trudy had stacked the day before. Copper grabbed at the nearest one with her teeth, and as it was surprisingly lightweight, she pulled it through the opening.

Using her nose, the greedy horse-cow nudged the carton up against the brick box and stepped onto it, carefully at first, testing it for support. As she transferred her weight onto her front hoof it broke through the cardboard lid exposing brightly coloured shiny paper. "These don't look like any eggs I've seen before, but they smell very nice." Delving inside the carton, she took out one of the boxes inside and shook it. The sides split and the shiny foil egg fell to the ground, breaking and exposing its brown shell. "How odd, no yolk," she said.

Still concerned about Roger's reluctance to interact with the group, Willow decided she would ask him what was wrong. She left the others at the fence and trotted over to the gate where Roger was standing.

"Roger, are you okay?" Willow asked.

"I've got something on my mind."

"What?"

"It's something I overheard Mr Neville say on his talking oblong a few days ago."

"What did you hear?"

"Mr Neville said, Mr O'Leary was thinking of getting rid of the cows, because we haven't produced any milk. So we're to be sold off for pet food."

"Pet food!" cried Willow.

"Mr Neville said he'd send Mr Clifford a thing called a text. I saw him do it this morning before he left and look what he's left behind on the gatepost."

Willow and Roger were looking at Mr Neville's talking oblong that was balanced on top of the gatepost. Suddenly it began to vibrate and play a thin sounding melody. The noise and the vibrations made it shake and the two friends watched as it bounced its way off the fencepost and into a patch of nettles; once hidden in the undergrowth, the music and vibrating stopped. Roger, not one to be afraid of the stinging weeds poked his head into the nettles and retrieved the talking oblong, gently putting it down on the ground. "The text is inside," he said.

"You seem to know quite a lot about the humans' talking oblongs. Do you know how they work?"

"No, because I'm a fucking donkey."

"Let's take it to the others; maybe someone will know what to do?"

Willow and Roger wandered down the field to the horse-cows looking over the fence, "What do you have there?" asked Chestnut.

"It's Mr Neville's talking oblong," said Willow. "It has an important thing called a text hidden inside."

"Do you know how to work it?" asked Bramble.

"No, because I'm a fucking pony."

Applejack turned his attention away from the flashing lights and human activity over the fence. The morning sunshine reflected in his eyes, making them flash orange, and at that moment Willow thought he looked rather handsome. "What's going on?" he asked.

Chestnut explained what was happening, telling him that Willow had said that there was an important thing called a text locked inside Mr Neville's talking oblong. When Applejack had asked him if Willow knew how to retrieve the text, Chestnut explained that she didn't, because she was a fucking pony."

"Maybe you press one of these little pads," Bramble said and with her soft nose, she nudged the talking oblong. Immediately it sprung into life and the pads lit up, making the five horse-cows step back in fright.

"Hello?" a small voice said, "is anyone there?"

"Where's that sound coming from?" Bramble asked.

"The talking oblong," said Roger.

"Shush," said Willow. "Let's listen."

So, six pairs of ears listened as the voice spoke again. "Can you hear me? This is the vet, are you there?" There was a pause before the voice spoke again "Just tell your boss I've checked and yes he can keep alpacas in the field. Tell him I know someone with a small trailer who can deliver them for him, but only one at a time. Oh, and tell him I'll collect the cows for slaughter on Tuesday."

"Tuesday," shrieked Bramble.

"Slaughter," said Applejack.

"Shit," said Roger.

"Shush," said Willow. "Chestnut, what day is it today?"

"I don't know, you see I'm a..."

"Yes, we know," the others said in agreement.

Just then the voice said, "Forget Tuesday, I'll be over tomorrow morning."

"There's only one thing for it," said Willow.

"What that?" Applejack asked.

"There's some furry white cloth in the back of the stable, I'll have to make us all an alpaca suit."

"Do you know what an alpaca is?" said Chestnut.

"Of course she doesn't," said Bramble. "She's a fucking pony."

"Well, actually, yes I do. The alpaca is a domesticated South American species of camelid, often confused with the llama due to their similarity in appearance."

"Well then, I think it's another splendid idea," said Chestnut.

The horse-cows' discussion was disturbed by a scream and they looked up to see Miss Trudy outside the brick box with the square glass eye, with Copper skulking down the field, keeping close to the hedge. Willow picked up Mr Neville's talking oblong and trotted over to where Miss Trudy was picking shiny pieces of coloured paper out of the grass. Willow placed the talking oblong delicately onto a clump of clover and stepped aside. "Someone has broken in and eaten a whole sodding box of Easter eggs," screeched Miss Trudy.

"Look on the bright side," said Mr Neville, bending down.

"Bright side?" she said, screeching again.

"At least I've found my phone."

That night as the others slept, Willow used her scissors to cut out the white furry fabric and sat at the cloth-joining machine making the alpaca disguises.

As the birds began to sing, heralding the arrival of the new day, she had at last finished the final outfit. Half asleep, she managed to crawl into her bed just as Mr Neville opened the stable doors.

Copper was the first out of the door, eager to get started on her breakfast. She began trotting up to the feeding trough, however, when she saw the cage on wheels at the gate, she turned around and galloped back to the stable. "Bad news," she called. "News, that's worse than bad."

"What is it?" said Chestnut.

"There's a cage on wheels at the gate, the humans must be ready to take us away."

"Don't panic," said Willow. "Where's Mr Neville?"

"Down at the bottom of the field."

"Good. Okay everyone I have a plan. The voice inside the talking oblong said the alpacas can only be delivered one at a time.

"So, here's what we'll do, we'll all go outside and one at a time we come back into the stable to get changed. That way, if Mr Neville sees us, he'll think that one of the alpacas has been delivered and one of the cows has been taken away."

"You're so clever," said Bramble. "Who shall get changed first?"

"I think our old friend Chestnut," said Applejack.

"How kind," said Chestnut, who remained inside as the others walked out into the field. He quickly stepped out of his cow disguise and into the alpaca outfit, before strolling outside, joining his friends.

After Applejack and Roger had also changed into their outfits, Mr Neville looked up and saw three alpacas and three cows. "Bugger me," he said to himself. Because occasionally he could be rather uncouth. "I've been so busy; I never even noticed that three of those South American things had been delivered already." Not only was Mr Neville sometimes uncouth, but he was also rather dim.

Bramble quickly changed, closely followed by Willow. "Your turn," she said to Copper.

Just as Copper was about to change into her alpaca suit, a box on wheels arrived at the gate, and out of its inside stepped the vet. "Morning," called Mr Neville, and then under his breath he added, "You money-grabbing piece of shit."

The horse-cows, or rather as they were now, the horse-alpacas started to panic. "Quickly Copper, hurry up," said Willow. "Here let me help you." Using her teeth Willow grabbed at the zip and tugged.

"It's the zip, it's stuck," moaned Copper.

"Oh dear, you've put on so much weight you've jammed it."

Bramble came to help Willow as Copper struggled to get free but she'd become such a fatty lately that she was well and truly stuck fast inside her cow suit.

"Ah, look at those two alpacas having fun with the last remaining cow," said Mr Neville.

"I'll put a halter on her," said Mr Clifford, and very quickly he had Copper in harness and was leading her up the field, past the big tree and towards the gate, where the cage on wheels stood.

The five remaining horse-alpacas stood in horror as they watched Mr Clifford, the money-grabbing piece of shit, load Copper inside the cage and close the door behind her. And in silence, as the boxes on wheels left, they watched as their friend melted into the distance.

No one spoke of Copper ever again.

Chapter Three: The Silver Box

One day, three men arrived at the field in a fat white box on wheels, the men had come to work and there had been much noise from hammering, swearing and the erecting of several new signs. Willow had heard Mr O'Leary say that the new signs would attract other humans to come and visit the field; nevertheless, despite this activity, no one came.

Eight weeks passed, and some of the horse-alpacas were growing more irritable with each coming day; their disguises were incredibly itchy, and the furry fabric became more uncomfortable as the temperature rose with the approach of summer.

One June morning as Bramble and Willow were standing beneath the big tree, taking shelter from the sun, Chestnut ambled over. "It's going to be another warm day," he said.

"Looks like it," said Willow.

"I hate it," moaned Bramble. "I wish I could take this bloody stupid outfit off, even if just for a few minutes."

"Remember what happened to Copper," old Chestnut said. "We must stay safe. I don't think it would be wise to slip out of our disguises for even a minute's respite from the heat. Get yourselves into the stable, it's cooler inside." The horse-alpacas nodded and followed their old friend into the sagging wooden building; although Willow was certain even the cool of the stable wouldn't do much to quell Bramble's mood.

Applejack was snoozing in the corner; his head resting on a discarded straw bale, across from him sat Roger the donkey, his eyes heavy with mid-morning sleep. "Morning," Willow said, as she entered the stable, "It's warm and sunny again."

"You don't say," Roger said; grumpy as usual. "I'd never have guessed the reason I'm sweating like a junkie trapped inside a pharmacy is due to the weather."

"Oh shut up, you miserable little shit," said Bramble.

"Do you mind?" brayed Roger.

"Not really."

Willow was about to step in to avert any potential argument but held her tongue as the humans appeared at the stable door.

"Useless," Mr O'Leary said, "bloody useless, not one sodding visitor has come to see these bloody alpaca. All that money spent on putting up the new signage, wasted."

"Maybe we could take out an advert in the local paper," said Mr Neville, offering a simple solution to Mr O'Leary's problem of non-existent tourism."

"And maybe you could shut your fat useless mouth." You see like Roger he was also a miserable little shit. "I've had an idea. What we need is something exciting. Something that will bring in the visitors, all hoping to part with their money for a thrilling day out." Mr O'Leary held up a silver disc. "What we need is this."

"A DVD?"

"No, you idiot, not a DVD. What you're about to see is the future."

The horse-alpacas, Roger the donkey-alpaca and Mr Neville watched as Mr O'Leary took a small silver box from the inside of his coat, which quite frankly had seen better days, and could have done with a good wash on a hot cycle. (The coat that is, not the silver box, which was quite new.)

The lid of the silver box sprang up and Mr O'Leary placed the disc inside. There was a whirring noise and after using one of his dirt-stained fingers to press a button, music began to play. Images flashed across the screen, children running and jumping. Open topped boxes on wheels raced along metal tracks, looping and twisting as the humans that were sat inside held their arms up in the air as if supporting an imaginary beam. Willow enjoyed the sound of humans having a good time; their squeals and laughter filled the stable. Suddenly a loud roar exploded from the silver box, making the horse-alpacas jump, and causing old Chestnut to fart loudly.

"Wow, what a brilliant idea," said Mr Neville, "but what will happen to the alpacas?"

"We'll get rid. I'll call the vet. The money-grabbing bastard will know what to do with them. But that can wait until later. I need you to give me a hand outside."

The Humans left the stable and the horse-alpacas gathered around the silver box. "What did Mr O'Leary call the thing inside?" Applejack asked.

"A DVD," said Willow as she crept forward and sniffed at the silver box. "Humans use them to watch films and videos that have been embedded into the disc. DVD stands for digital versatile disc."

"And I bet you're now going to tell us that you know how to get the film to play on the silver box?" muttered Roger.

"No, because I'm a fucking pony."

"Is there an instruction manual, maybe that will help?" said Bramble.

"And will you be able to follow the instructions?" Chestnut asked.

"No, because I'm also a fucking pony."

"What happens if I press this button?" Applejack asked.

"How the bloody hell do I know," said Roger. "I'm a fucking donkey."

"Press it," Bramble said. She's obviously in an impish mood, thought Willow; but that said there's often a fine line between impish behaviour and bullying. "I'm not sure I should," the dappled horse-alpaca said.

"Go on Applejack, press it," urged Bramble.

"Maybe you shouldn't," Chestnut said. "You might break it."

"Oh, for fucks sake," Roger said, "Just press the sodding button."

Applejack nudged the button with his nose, and as if by magic once again music and pictures appeared on the screen. The horse-alpacas watched in wonderment until the final roar echoed around the stable once again. This time, aware that the roar was coming, Chestnut didn't fart.

That evening after Mr Neville had made sure the horse-alpacas were safely shut away for the night; they settled down in their stalls and tried to sleep. The evening was warm, and the air inside their stable became an oppressive mix of exhaust fumes from the motorway and old straw.

Willow in particular was having trouble getting to sleep; the film she had watched that afternoon was playing on her mind. She looked across at Bramble, who was resting on her side; her white eyelids were fringed by long dark kohl-coloured eyelashes, and as the eyes beneath them moved, they fluttered like piebald butterflies.

Roger was standing looking up and out of the open window; Willow wondered if the little donkey was looking at the stars when Applejack walked across the stable towards him. "You look pensive," Applejack said to him. "Pensive," said Roger, "Pensive, who the fuck says, pensive? You can be a right pretentious prat sometimes Applejack."

"Okay, you miserable little sod; you look lost in thought?"

"Screw you," said Roger.

"Everything, okay?" Willow called across the stable.

"It's just Roger; being his usual grumpy self."

"Ignore him, he's just a moody twat, I reckon he suffers from little man syndrome," said Bramble, not bothering to open her eyes.

"Little man syndrome?"

"Yes." Bramble shifted position, her slender forelegs stretching out before her. "Short men are always officious little prats, and Roger's no different. He's just jealous because he's not a handsome dappled horse with fine fetlocks like you are."

"You're right; he's just a short-arsed little donkey."

"I can hear you, you know," scowled Roger, but his words were lost as Chestnut farted loudly. "Chestnut!" everyone chimed.

"Sorry," the old horse-alpaca said. "It's just come to me."

"What has come to you?" Applejack asked.

"Mr O'Leary's new plan; everyone, quickly gather around."

With the exception of Roger, the horse-alpacas gathered around the old Shire; no one wanting to be too close to his backside for fear of him blowing off again. Bramble rested her chin upon a dainty hoof as he began to tell them a tale. "Long ago and oh so far away."

"I fell in love with you before the second show," sang Roger sarcastically: He was abruptly shushed by the others.

Chestnut snorted his displeasure and turned around in his stall before clearing his throat in readiness to continue with his story. "Long ago, before I came here I worked on a large estate, it wasn't doing very well and the number of human visitors began to dwindle. The estate owner had the idea to bring in something exotic to tempt the humans to part with that paper they call money."

"What exotic thing did the owner bring in?" Applejack asked.

"Big cats," said Chestnut.

"How big," Roger sneered. "Gargantuan ginger toms, obese tabbies?"

"Some so big they could easily wrestle a small pony to the ground."

"What were these cats like?" asked Willow.

"Ferocious," Chestnut said, "There was talk among the animals on the estate that in a far off land called Africa, these cats were the killers of striped horses."

"So, Mr O'Leary wants to bring these ferocious cats to our field in an attempt to get the humans to visit and give him their paper money?"

"Exactly, and although my memory isn't what it once was, I remember that the animal we saw today on the talking picture disc is called a lion."

"What shall we do now? If what Chestnut tells us is true, surely we'll all be killed by these lions," Bramble sighed.

"Oh I know what we can do;" piped up Roger derisively, "Willow can make us all lion suits."

"Good idea," said Bramble.

"I was only joking. I'm bored with all this dressing up."

"Oh, go stick it up your arse," Willow said; amazing herself with her rudeness. "When I was sewing the alpaca suits, I found a shaggy brown rug. It was being used to cover up some tins of that foul smelling liquid that Mr Neville uses on the fence posts. If we cut out strips of the rug, we can make shaggy collars and then I can fix them onto the alpaca outfits and we'll look like lions. Applejack, do you know how to use a pair of scissors?"

"Of course not, I'm a fucking horse."

"Isn't there one thing you've overlooked?" said Roger.

"What?"

"These bloody alpaca suits are white and the lions in the film were a sandy colour."

"Oh yes," Willow shrugged. "I didn't think about that."

"I know," said an excited Bramble. "If we take our disguises off now, we could colour them with the liquid Mr Neville uses on the fence posts and hang them up to dry in the warm night air."

So with the others sleeping, Willow made shaggy collars and Bramble dipped the alpaca outfits in the noxious liquid, which smelled so bad that it masked the stench coming from the regular explosions of hot air from Chestnut's bottom.

***

The next morning the horses were woken by such a commotion outside. Gingerly Willow popped her head out of the stable door to see Mr Clifford, the money-grabbing bastard at the gate with his box on wheels, linked to it was a cage; it was similar to the one that had taken Copper away weeks before and inside the cage were four snarling lions.

Willow watched as Mr Clifford poked a stick through the bars of the cage, tormenting one of the big cats inside. You see despite being a vet, he was also a cruel twat. Mr Clifford laughed at the angry yellow feline as it roared its annoyance; the sound from the large cat vibrated in the air and Bramble almost whinnied with fright.

"Morning," said Mr Neville, "Are these the cats?"

"No," said Mr Clifford, "They're fucking elephants." You see not only was he cruel, and a money-grabbing bastard, he was also crap when it came to attempts at humour. "How many are we having?"

"Four. So can you sort it out while I go for a pee behind that tree?"

"Quickly," Willow said, "There's no time to delay. Hurry everyone, get into your lion suits." The horses all changed quickly and stepped outside of the stable.

Roger hadn't bothered to put his new disguise on and was standing apart from the others; all of whom looked resplendent in their lion get-ups. "Hurry up you silly old donkey," said Bramble. "Get dressed; Mr Neville, will be opening the gate soon to let in the lions."

"Don't want to," moaned the donkey.

"But you must," Chestnut told him.

"I don't have to do anything of the sort; I'm fed up with these silly games."

"What's that frigging donkey doing in there?" Mr Clifford said coming around the tree he'd just peed up. "Get it out of there before those four lions rip it to shreds."

"What lions?" said Mr Neville, turning around to see four lions standing near the stable and a donkey standing near the big tree.

"Just do it," shouted Mr Clifford.

"Roger," Willow mouthed silently as she watched her friend; albeit a grumpy one being led away by Mr Neville.

At the gate, Mr Clifford counted four lions inside the field, scratched his bollocks, then his head and counted four lions inside the cage. Proving that despite being an animal medical professional, who had spent many years studying at veterinary college, he was in essence, quite stupid.

The four horse-lions spent the remainder of the day looking over the fence, watching the boxes on wheels travel along the M6. Some boxes navigated their way around the bumpy hole successfully, while others dipped in and out of the scar on the motorway's surface.

No one said a word, until bedtime that night, when Applejack said, "I know he was a miserable twat, but I think we shall all miss Roger."

Everyone agreed, and as sleep took them each in turn, Chestnut rolled over and farted.

Chapter Four: Cheese

Men in suits had been visiting the field all week, they came to shake their heads and wag their fingers. Every visit by the men in suits caused Mr O'Leary's face to go red and he'd shout and swear, before clipping Mr Neville around the back of the head.

During the last visit, Willow had heard the men in suits use a word she had never heard before. That word was, prosecute.

So one fine morning, after breakfast she sidled over to Chestnut, who was standing beneath the big tree and asked him what the word meant.

"I'm not sure," replied her ancient friend, "but it sounds like an important word."

"Do you think, Applejack will know?"

"I doubt it because he's a fucking horse."

Shrouded in the shadow of the big tree, the two horse-lions watched Mr Neville working at the top of the field, he was carrying big round things into the brick box with the square glass eye. The round things clanged like bells as Mr Neville half dropped, half put them down upon the stone floor.

Willow was just about to ask her friend if he knew what the round things could be when she was distracted by a loud whistle. She turned to look in the direction of the sound and saw Miss Trudy walking towards the field. "Sexy pants where are you?" she called as she neared the gate.

"Over here in the sodding lock-up," Mr Neville replied.

"I wonder what, she wants?" Chestnut said.

"She probably wants to suck Mr Neville's face again." Willow caught a glimpse of the old Shire's fetlocks as they quivered with disgust, "How revolting, I do hate it when the humans suck at each other's faces."

Willow watched as Miss Trudy balanced her heavy bosoms on the top of the gate. "Is it safe to come in?"

"Yes. The lions won't bother with you," said Mr Neville stepping out of the brick box with the square glass eye. "To be honest they're lazy buggers."

Mr Neville's girlfriend opened the gate and stepped into the field, "Is there anything I can do to help?"

"Yes, you could get over here and snog my face off."

***

Applejack wandered over to join his friends under the big tree. As he strolled up the field, Willow thought he had a rather lovely way of walking, elegant and refined yet still strong and masculine.

"Good morning," said Chestnut. "Willow and I were just wondering what those round clanging things are for?"

"I heard him earlier talking to Mr O'Leary, he said they're for making past your eyes cheese."

"Past your eyes cheese?" said Willow. "That sounds odd."

"Oh dear," muttered Chestnut. "They're at it again." The three horse-lions looked over to see the humans sucking each other's faces. "Look, his hands must be cold," said Willow.

"Why do you say that?"

"He's put them up Miss Trudy's jumper."

As the humans went inside the brick box with the square glass eye and closed the door, the three horse-lions started to walk down the field and away from the big tree. They had barely reached the fence at the bottom of the field, when the sound of gravel pinging against the gate made them turn around, to see the vet's green box on wheels arrive. The doors to the green box opened and Mr O'Leary and Mr Clifford climbed out.

Bramble trotted over to join the three horse-lions and together they all watched as Mr O'Leary walked over to the brick box with the square glass eye; as he went inside Chestnut said, "Oh dear."

The horse-lions burst out laughing as Mr Neville emerged from the doorway chased by Mr O'Leary, who had a face that was as red as a robin's breast.

"I wonder where Mr Neville's trousers have gone?" said Bramble.

"It must have been hot inside," said Willow.

"What makes you say that?"

"Because Miss Trudy's just come out red-faced, and she's got no jumper on."

Willow thought Mr Clifford had an odd look on his face, a sort of smirk as he watched Miss Trudy pulling her jumper back on. "Nice tits," he said.

"Piss off," spat Miss Trudy. Because you see Mr Clifford was also a sleazy piece of shit - according to Mr O'Leary, who had been overheard saying it to Mr Neville.

Miss Trudy walked away with Mr Clifford calling after her; Willow wondered if his words had been blown away on the breeze, as she couldn't catch what he had said. Chestnut however told her that he thought Miss Trudy must have heard what the vet had said, as she had turned around and given him the two-fingered gesture.

"I bet they were doing that human body rubbing thing," said Bramble.

"I can't see what pleasure they get out of it," said Applejack.

"Could be like rubbing your neck against a fence post," said Chestnut.

"Oooh," the three other horse-lions said in unity; having all enjoyed a neck rub against a fence post in the past.

"There's always strange goings on with humans," said Willow.

Later that evening as the four horse-lions settled down inside the stable, Chestnut asked if Bramble had been told about the other strange goings-on that day. "What goings on?" the white filly asked.

Applejack stepped forward. In the safety of the stable, he had rolled back his attire, revealing his marble-coloured head. Willow thought that his profile in the moonlight was rather dashing, the grey of his coat complimented by the pearlescent light of the moon. "All morning Mr Neville has been taking round things into the brick box," the dappled horse said.

"What sort of things?"

"Round, metal looking tubs."

"I heard Mr Neville say they were for something called past your eyes cheese. I bet they'll be seeing windows for human faces that have been made from cheese?"

"Don't be silly," sniped Bramble. "Are the drum things made of a similar material to our water trough?"

"Yes."

"Then, I know what they are, they're not for past your eyes cheese."

"What are they for then?" said Willow.

"They are used to pasteurise milk, it's something farmers do when they make cheese."

"Make cheese?"

"Yes, before I came here, I lived near a farm where they made cheese."

"But what would Mr O'Leary want with cheese making things?"

"That's what we need to find out," Bramble replied snootily. Because sometimes she could be a right uppity little bitch. "I think that tomorrow, one of us should make it our duty to investigate and find out what's going on," said Chestnut, as he lowered himself down onto the bed of straw in his stall.

"I'll do it, I'll do it," whinnied Bramble. "I am, after all the clever one, when it comes to knowing about cheese."

"Show off," mumbled Willow.

"Snotty bitch," whispered Applejack.

"Very well," said Chestnut, "Goodnight everyone."

Before any of the others had a chance to respond, he drifted off to sleep and began to snore loudly.

***

The following morning, Mr Neville made what he often referred to as a flying visit to the field, he opened the stable doors, filled the manger and replenished the water trough before leaving again.

The horse-lions gathered at the bottom of the field, by the fence that overlooked the motorway. Willow was intrigued by a long tube on wheels that had many glass eyes down its side. Inside the tube, humans were sitting in two layers, one on top of the other and the smaller ones were smiling and waving to her; they all looked very happy she thought and hiding it from the other horse-lions she waved back.

As the tube on wheels continued on its journey down the motorway, a pair of blackbirds began dancing across the top of the fence. Willow turned around and in the distance, she saw Chestnut browsing on a piece of couch grass and thought, what an odd sight it is, to see a lion eating grass.

The day passed slowly as the horse-lions waited for an opportunity to arise, enabling Bramble to engage in the proposed surveillance of the humans. Late afternoon and just as they were sure that no chance would arrive, the sound of boxes on wheels, followed by voices indicated an opportunity.

At the top of the field, Mr Clifford was talking to Mr Neville. "Look Mr Neville has returned, and he's talking to the vet," Willow said to Bramble. "Go and see what you can find out."

As Bramble trotted up the field, Willow was sure that the white filly would enjoy feeling important. She hoped that this wouldn't mean the young pony would become unbearable, as she often did, especially when she felt superior to the others. "How do you think she's doing?" asked Chestnut, joining Willow.

"She's loitering around the base of the big tree, I do hope she's not too far away to hear what the humans are saying."

"Oh look, Mr Clifford is speaking into his talking oblong."

"I have learned that the humans call the thing that he's doing, making a telephone call."

"Well done Willow, I sometimes wonder what we would do without you."

Willow started to enjoy the sensation of feeling superior, however, it was short-lived as she saw Bramble walking back down the field in her direction. "So did you hear anything important?" asked Chestnut.

"Oh yes, very important. Very important indeed, in fact, I'd hazard a guess that what I heard could be…"

"Oh do stop wittering," Willow said. "What did you hear?"

"Mr Clifford told Mr Neville, that because Mr O'Leary didn't have a wild animal licence, he'd get prosecuted."

"There's that word again," said Chestnut.

"Yes apparently it means, someone could instigate legal action against Mr O'Leary, and he may get into terrible trouble," said Bramble.

"So what's going to happen?"

"He has to get rid of the mangy lions. Mr Clifford's words, not mine."

"Mangy," exclaimed Willow, rather put out. "Mangy. I'm rather proud of these outfits. I'd like to see him do a better job. In fact, I'd like to see him cut out fabric by the light of the moon and fasten it together during the night on an old cloth-joining machine in the back of a stable."

Willow had her rant and then looked over at the others who had waited patiently for her to finish. Bramble continued with her story. "Mr Clifford said he had contacts."

"We saw him use his talking oblong," said Chestnut.

"Yes, he spoke to Mr O'Leary."

"I wonder what he said."

"Who, Mr Clifford or Mr O'Leary?"

"Mr O'Leary, of course," said Willow, trying hard to keep the annoyance she was feeling in check.

"I know what he said, because he spoke about it with Mr Neville," Bramble sniped.

"And what did he say?"

"Who, Mr Neville or Mr Clifford?"

"Stop pissing about and just tell us," said Chestnut; he hadn't made any attempt to disguise his annoyance, thought Willow. "Mr O'Leary said Mr Clifford must come over tomorrow morning and dispatch the lions."

"Dispatch?"

"Yes, he said the vet was to come over and shoot them."

"Did he mention anything about cheese?" said Chestnut.

"No. Not a thing."

"Oh well. I guess it doesn't matter much now, not if we're all going to be killed in the morning."

That night after Mr Neville had left, and with conversation the furthest thing from the horse-lions minds, the last remnants of the day expired. Unhurriedly and noiselessly the night took over, and four pairs of eyes remained open, staring into the treacle heavy blackness.

Chapter Five: Joshua-James

As the new day began, the horse-lions spoke for the first time since settling down the previous evening. "I've been thinking," said Applejack. "If Mr Clifford is coming today to shoot the lions, why don't we save him a job?"

"I don't understand," said Bramble.

"If we take off our lion suits, then there'll be no lions to shoot."

"Oh yes."

"It wouldn't help," said Chestnut shaking his head. "Horses or lions, Mr O'Leary will still want to put us to sleep. Remember why we started dressing up in the first place."

"It was a good idea though," said Willow, giving Applejack a friendly snort.

Mr Neville opened the stable doors as he usually did, but this day felt different, "Good morning my lovelies," said Miss Trudy, as she popped her head around the door. "It's a lovely sunny day today." Willow could detect a hint of sadness in the human's voice, it was almost as if she was trying to say everything was nice when in reality it was a little bit shit

Applejack and Bramble were the first to leave the stable, followed by old Chestnut: as it took the aged Shire a little longer with each coming day to ease his old bones into action. Willow however didn't move she remained on her bed of straw. Mr Neville walked over and ran his hand through her mane. "I think I'll miss you the most," he said tickling her behind her ears.

"I wish there was another way," said Miss Trudy.

"So do I, but the vet is on his way over already."

"But they're such lovely big cats. It's a shame to have to destroy them."

"I know." Mr Neville's voice cracked as he replied and Willow looked up to see that his eyes were leaking. Sensing he was feeling sad, she nudged him with her nose and did her best to simulate a cat-like purr. This was her way of letting him know, that she understood how he felt.

"When are the goats coming?"

Goats? thought Willow.

"They're arriving tomorrow."

Goats, of course, it all makes sense now. Stretching and loudly yawning the horse-lion rose from her bed and padded out of the stable eager to tell the others what she had just heard.

The other horse-lions were standing underneath the big tree, sheltering from the morning sun, when Willow joined them. "I think I've solved the cheese mystery."

"And will it postpone our inevitable demise?" asked Chestnut.

"I'm not sure."

"So!" said Bramble sharply. "Let's hear it then." She was obviously put out that Willow had discovered what she had failed to do.

"I overheard Mr Neville and Miss Trudy talking, they said that Mr O'Leary was getting some goats tomorrow."

"Of course," said Applejack, "and the goats will produce the milk for making cheese."

"I don't see how knowing this will help us," said Bramble.

"There's an old hosepipe in the stable. If I take the lion manes that I made, off these suits, I could then use the hose to make horns and when they're fixed onto our old alpaca outfits, we'll look like goats."

"But aren't you forgetting one thing, Mr Clifford is coming today to…" Before Bramble could finish her sentence, the vet's green box on wheels arrived at the gate. "It looks like we're too late."

"Bollocks and buggery," said Chestnut. "If only there had been some way to delay his arrival."

The horse-lions watched as the vet climbed out of his box on wheels. There seemed to be much discussion between the three humans before Mr Neville and Miss Trudy broke away and walked slowly down the field towards the friends gathered under the big tree.

"Come on lard-arse," shouted Mr Clifford, "I haven't got all day."

"Go fuck yourself," Miss Trudy called back, followed by the middle figure gesture.

Mr Neville walked over to Applejack and patted his rump. Willow thought that her handsome grey friend looked nervous. Maybe being chosen first to take a bullet had made him feel a tad uncomfortable.

She was watching as Mr Clifford took the loud-bang shooting stick out of its cover when a new voice called out, "I say, you man there."

At the gate, a very fine box on wheels with a miniature leaping cat fixed to its front had stopped and out had climbed two humans, a grown female one and a small boy one. They were both dressed in tan-coloured corduroy jeans that were twinned with green padded jackets. "I say. Are you open?" asked the female.

"Well... we…" Miss Trudy, put her hand on her boyfriend's shoulder, silencing his stammering. "Can I help?"

"Yes, I was driving past and thought I'd bring my son, Joshua-James to see the lions of Walsall."

"What do you think is happening?" said Bramble.

"I think," said Willow, "it may just be that delay Chestnut was talking about."

Mr Clifford stormed over, his face the colour of poppies. He moved in close to Mr Neville and rather rudely thought Willow, barked at him. "Just as soon as you get rid of those people the sooner I can shoot your tatty old lions."

"But, they've come here to see them, we can't disappoint them."

"I haven't got time for this; I'm needed back at the surgery in an hour." The vet pushed past Mr Neville and strode over to the gate. "Madam, I'm afraid the lions are all about to be put down, therefore I suggest you leave now; that is if you don't want your son to see them shot."

As Mr Clifford spoke to the woman, again quite rudely thought Willow, the small boy leaned over the gate and looked directly into her brown eyes and said, "What a manky looking lion you are."

"Don't be so horrid Joshua-James," said the boy's mother, before turning to Miss Trudy. "Is it safe to be this close to them?"

"Perfectly, this particular lion's very gentle."

"Come along ladies, I don't have time to stand around while you two gossip, I need to get these lions dispatched."

"Isn't there any chance you could do it later, it won't do any harm to let these people have a morning watching them," said Miss Trudy as she took the vet by the arm and led him away from the visitor's ears.

"No, I'm sorry, I have appointments all afternoon, so it has to be now or never." With their backs to the gate, Miss Trudy and the vet failed to notice that Joshua-James had climbed over the gate. The boy grabbed Willow by her tail and yanked at it. Surprised the horse-lion spun around as the boy picked up a stick and poked her on the nose. "So you want to play those games do you?" she said.

"What?" Joshua-James stood wide-eyed. "Did you just speak?"

Willow suddenly realised she may have found a way to buy them all some more time, "Okay short-arse, you asked for this." She roared and grabbed at the jacket that Joshua-James was wearing and very quickly she dragged the small boy through a gap in the hedge that led into the next field. Willow ran across the grass, putting some distance between herself and the humans. She dropped the yelping boy and using her nose she nudged him, urging him to run away, but he just lay upon the grass staring up at her, his mouth wide with fear. "Come on run you daft bugger," she said.

"Fuck me, a talking lion."

"Watch your language you little shit; now do me a favour and run."

The boy clambered to his feet and ran, Mr Neville and Miss Trudy gave chase, while the vet did absolutely nothing and the mother remained at the gate, wailing like a cat on heat.

The boy zigged and zagged across the field as Willow pursued him making sure that she was always several steps behind. Suddenly the boy stumbled and fell, feeling the humans on her tail the horse-lion was upon him in an instant. "No you don't," said Miss Trudy grabbing Willow by the scruff. "That's enough child chasing for today."

Mr Neville helped Joshua-James to his feet as his girlfriend led Willow away. "You gave us all a bit of a scare then."

Back at the gate Mr Neville spewed apologies as the woman threatened legal action. "There's no harm done, I think she was just playing," he said

"When you've quite finished," said Mr Clifford.

"I guess we'd better get started."

"I don't think so," the vet said snottily, "I don't have time now and I'm needed back at the surgery."

"What about tomorrow?"

"I can come out around five-thirty in the morning, but that'll incur an additional out-of-hours call-out fee."

"Very well, I'm sorry we've wasted your time today."

"Don't worry, you'll still be charged for today's debacle."

"I don't doubt it, you money-grabbing piece of filth."

"Sorry, what did you say?"

"Thanks, I'll see you in the morning."

As the vet left the field, Willow watched as Joshua-James's mother fussed over him. "The lion can speak," he said as his shirt was lifted to allow her to check his body for bites.

"Don't be silly Joshua-James."

"Honest, the lion can speak, I heard it."

"He's delirious," she said looking up at Miss Trudy.

"It could be shock."

"Shock! He's lucky to be alive."

"But mother, the lion can speak, it told me to run."

"I won't tell you again, I've never heard anything so absurd."

She dragged the boy towards her box on wheels and roughly pushed him inside. "And let me tell you," she turned to face Mr Neville, "if it wasn't for the fact that these dangerous beasts were going to be put down tomorrow, you'd be seeing me in court."

As the visitors' box on wheels disappeared around the bend in the lane, Miss Trudy whispered into Willow's ear, "It's a pity you didn't eat that snotty little shit, fancy calling you manky."

That evening Willow cut lengths of hosepipe and fashioned them into horns before trimming what was not needed from their now redundant bridles hanging on the walls. She secured the horns to the crownpieces and using Applejack as her model she demonstrated how to wear the horns. They sat upon the head where the crownpiece usually sits and the throatlatch held them in place. After removing the fake lion mane she cut holes in the fabric at the crown and the horns slid through, hiding the leather strap of the bridle. "I say," said Chestnut, "You make a very handsome goat."

"Thank you," said Applejack.

"I suggest we all turn in for the night, and tomorrow morning we can put our goat horns on before the humans arrive."

That evening satisfied with her endeavours Willow slept soundly and dreamt of a meadow full of wildflowers where she frolicked with Applejack as the sun shone high in a clear blue sky.

***

Before the wild birds had risen to welcome the new day with song, the sound of voices could be heard outside. Willow asked Chestnut to take a look, he popped his head out of the stable door and after retracting it quickly, he said, "Mr Neville and the vet are here."

"He's early," said Applejack.

"How do you know he's early?" said a sleepy Bramble. "Can you tell the time?"

"Of course not, I'm a fucking horse."

"Keep your mane on, moody arse." Bramble sighed, proving to everyone that she wasn't really what you could call, a morning pony.

"Quickly, everyone put your horns on." The old Shire said, showing as usual that he was good at taking charge and giving orders. He suggested that everyone help each other to put their goat horns on.

Bramble helped Willow into her horns and being the tallest, Applejack helped Chestnut. Very soon the horse-goats were ready, all except Bramble who, despite the protestations of the others had removed her goat disguise so that she could comb the scruffy beard that had been sewn onto the chin.

"Bramble quickly get back into your goat suit."

"I couldn't possibly be seen with an unkempt beard."

"This is not the time for vanity."

"Oh, so I'm vain, am I?"

"Bramble please," said Willow, "Let's not fall out, I beg you, please hurry up and put your disguise on."

"Very well, but I need this throatlatch slackening off, it's far too tight." She shook her head vigorously in an attempt to make the leather strap more accommodating when one of the horns fell off at the exact time that the stable doors opened. A shaft of early morning light filtered into the stable and fell upon the pretty white filly with the horn. "Bugger me," said Mr Neville.

"I'd rather not," said Mr Clifford, his eyes as large as satellite dishes. "I don't believe it, there's a fucking unicorn in the stable."

"Looks like the goats have been delivered and the lions have gone."

"Do you think the unicorn did it?" said the vet, who despite being a member of the Royal College of Veterinary Surgeons, couldn't tell the difference between a mythical beast and a white horse with a length of hose on its head.

"Don't be silly," said Mr Neville. "What do you mean, the unicorn did it?"

"Magic, that's what I mean."

"You know for an allegedly educated man, you do talk bollocks sometimes."

"Very well, if you think I'm talking bollocks, then you won't mind if I take the unicorn."

"Not at all, but don't blame me when you become the laughing stock of the veterinary world."

The horse-goats were ushered into the rear of the stable as Bramble was led away by the vet. "We must save her," said Willow, whispering through her beard. "There's nothing we can do," said Chestnut, "but hope that, that idiot of a vet realises that she's just a white pony before he loads her into the two-wheeled tall crate beside the gate."

Daybreak arrived, bringing with it birdsong as the early morning mist was burned from the field. Mr Neville returned after filling the feed trough and as he raked out the old straw in preparation to lay fresh, he said, "What with talking lions and unicorns, this has been one seriously bonkers twenty-four hours."

It didn't take long for the horse-goats to realise that Bramble would not be coming back.

Chapter Six: Lady Godiva

The horse-goats hadn't slept well. During the twilight hours, the motorway had been taken over by noisy humans. Humans in bright yellow waistcoats had been placing upside-down striped cones on the surface of the road. These orange and white cones seemed to be there to direct the few boxes on wheels that travelled in the early hours, away from the bumpy hole.

The field was bathed in acrid light that came from several three-legged poles that had brilliant stars on top of them, and this light shone through the cracks in the stable's wooden walls.

Unable to sleep, Willow had volunteered to go outside to investigate, and now as she squeezed back through the loose plank at the rear of the stable, she was glad to be back inside surrounded by the comforting smell of straw "What's going on out there?" said Applejack, as he let the loose plank he'd been holding open for his friend fall back into place.

"Humans," she said.

"What is that dreadful smell?" Chestnut said, his nose wrinkling.

"It's some steaming, black stuff that the humans are pouring onto the surface of the motorway."

Applejack lifted his nose aloft, and after taking a strident sniff at the air, said, "I quite like it."

"There's always one," said Chestnut. "I'm certain we'll never get to sleep with all this noise, not to mention the smell."

"When I looked over the fence," said Willow settling down on her bed of straw, "I saw a human wearing a yellow bowl on his head, he was scratching the motorway with what looked like a giant comb on the end of a stick, while another poured steaming treacle coloured liquid into the bumpy hole. I heard one of them call it asphalt."

"I heard Mr Neville say that Miss Trudy likes that," said Applejack.

"Really?"

"Yes, he was telling the vet, that she liked to get her ass felt."

Willow groaned, settled down and shifted uncomfortably, her goat attire was starting to chafe, and how she wished she could take it off at night, but knew to do so would be foolish. Very foolish indeed.

***

Later, that morning, the sound of hammering disturbed the horse-goats, waking them from their erratic slumber, destroying any chance of getting any quality sleep. Chestnut rose and stretched his timeworn limbs before walking to the door and pushing the top half open. He was just in time to see a box on wheels drive away. "There's a wooden thing nailed to the fence."

"A wooden thing?" said Willow. "What kind of wooden thing?"

"It looks like a sign, I think that…" Chestnut was interrupted by the familiar sound of Mr Neville's two-wheeled seat arriving outside. From inside the stable, the sound of the gate's squeaking hinges could be heard followed by out of tune whistling.

Over the open top of the door Mr Neville's face appeared, "Morning, do you ladies have any milk for me this morning?" he said as he opened the bottom of the door. You're going to be disappointed, thought Willow as she trotted past him heading up the field towards the gate.

Willow was standing, looking at the sign when Mr Neville joined her. He stroked the top of her head, tickling her behind the ears; she looked up to see him using one of his fingers to pick his nose, something Willow didn't enjoy seeing him do. The horse-goat studied his face, noting that he had a determined look.

"What do you think the words on the sign say?" said Applejack as he joined Chestnut at the manger. The old Shire looked up and glanced across at the sign, then turned his attention back to his breakfast. Then with a shrug and a mouthful of food, he turned to Applejack and said, "I haven't a clue. I can't read, because..."

"I know," his friend said, "because you're a fucking horse."

Willow watched as Mr Neville took the talking oblong out of his coat pocket, she inched closer to hear what he had to say. "How much?" There was a pause, before he then said, "Okay I'll see what I can do."

Hearing his name being called, Mr Neville put away his talking oblong and looked up. In the distance Miss Trudy was making her way along the footpath that led to the field, she waved to him and said, "What's going on?" pointing to the sign.

"Mr O'Leary's selling the field."

"Why?"

"Probably because he's fed up. Like the cows before them, these bloody goats have been useless."

"Still no milk?" Miss Trudy climbed over the stile, her ample rear brushing against the wooden posts. "Not a drop," said Mr Neville, his eyes transfixed by her buttocks as they passed over the opening in the fence.

The three horse-goats shuddered as the two humans locked lips and began to suck at each other's faces. Mr O'Leary's selling the field, thought Willow, this will surely be the end of our deception now. As the humans parted, she made a decision that for the time being she'd keep her thoughts to herself.

"What's that?" said Mr Neville pointing to the giant pink sausage that his girlfriend had tucked under her arm. "It's fabric. I've got to make the Fancy-dress costumes for Cher's hen night."

"Cher?"

"You know, my mate that works at the retirement village up the road."

"So, what sort of costumes will you be making?"

"Well, because she lives in Coventry, we've decided to go out dressed as Lady Godiva. I'm making us all-in-ones. Body suits that will make it look like we're naked; it's going to be a right laugh. I thought I could use the sewing machine in the old tack room at the back of the stable."

"And do I get to see you model one of them when they're finished?"

"We'll see; saucy." She gave him a peck on the cheek, turned and strode away towards the stable.

As Miss Trudy started to work the rain came and the horse-goats sheltered inside. The repetitive sound of the sewing machine, coupled with the lack of sleep forced Chestnut's eyelids to close, and alongside his quiescent friends, the old horse-goat began to snore.

Later, refreshed from a few hours of sleep the horse-goats were woken by a smiling Mr Neville walking into the stable. Willow thought maybe he'd gone mad, as she had never seen his face feature such a wide grin before, it almost cut his chubby face in two. "Nearly finished, just one more seam to stitch," Miss Trudy called, looking up from the machine and through the door that led to the stalls. "You look happy."

"I am."

"Why?"

"Because I'm going to buy the field," he said beaming.

"Can you afford it?"

"I've spoken to Mr O'Leary, and he's agreed to let me pay him in monthly instalments after I've given him a deposit."

"And what will you do with it?" Miss Trudy cut the last thread and stood, shaking out the costume she had made. "I'm going to get myself some pigs and fatten them up for Easter next year."

"What about the goats, what will you do with them?"

"Mr O'Leary says I can do whatever I want with them, so I'll see if I can do a swap for some pigs." Picking up one of the flesh-coloured fancy-dress costumes Mr Neville looked at his girlfriend and said, "Well."

"Well, what?"

"Are you going to try one on for me?"

"But, I'd have to take all my clothes off first," she told him coquettishly. Which to be honest didn't suit a girl who spent her life lumbering about Wolverhampton dressed in black leggings and an oversized T-shirt.

Mr Neville watched as she began taking off her clothes, and another strange grin appeared. Willow noticed the front of his tracksuit bottoms now stuck out like a tent pitched on a vertical hillside and decided it was probably best to look away before they did the strange naked, body bouncing she had seen them do once before.

***

Over the next few days, Mr Neville started to make repairs to the old stable block, the paint-peeling doors were replaced with new ones and even the old ladder up to the hay loft was replaced.

Willow had become excited with a delivery of straw that had arrived and couldn't wait for it to become new, fresh bedding. She had later been upset after Chestnut had told her, the reason it was still baled up was because it wasn't for them but for the pigs that Mr Neville was hoping to replace them with. "Very well," said Willow. "I'll make us all a pig disguise.

"How?"

"I'll use the remnants of pink fabric that Miss Trudy has left behind."

"You are a clever pony," said Chestnut. "I'll let Applejack know of your idea."

With her friends outside enjoying the September sunshine, Willow collected the scraps of flesh-coloured cloth and laid them out on the stable floor, she took out her tape measure and scissors and began cutting shapes out.

That evening after their stable had been made secure and the humans had left the field, she sat at the cloth-joining machine and began sewing the shapes together.

As Willow worked, the night dissolved away like butter on a toasted crumpet and very soon the first creamy fingers of dawn were creeping under the stable door. The other horse-goats woke just as Mr Neville opened the doors.

Willow stretched, glad to be standing after many hours sat hunched over the bobbing pointy thing. She stepped outside and let the early sunshine warm her aching limbs. The sight of a human man at the top of the field caught her attention and she went to investigate. She stopped at the big tree and watched from a distance as he removed the sign that had been nailed onto the fence. The man asked who had purchased the field, and with his chest puffed up, Mr Neville had proudly told him, he had; he also discussed his plans for the field's future, which Willow overheard.

The two remaining horse-goats joined Willow beneath the big tree, and she told them that she had heard Mr Neville tell the sign-removing human that he'd found someone who wanted to swap some pigs for some goats. "When is this exchange going to take place?" asked Chestnut.

"I heard him say that the pigs will be delivered tomorrow."

"Tomorrow, oh dear."

"There's nothing to worry about," said Willow, reassuring her friends. "I've already finished two of the outfits, it will only take a short while to complete the other one. When the stable doors open tomorrow there'll be three pigs waiting inside."

***

The next morning the sound of the two-wheeled seat woke the horse-goats. "Quickly," said Applejack. "There's no time to waste, we need to put our pig suits on."

The three horse-goats rushed to change, Willow and Applejack were out of their goat suits and into the new pig ones but Chestnut was struggling with his goat disguise. "Damn, these frigging buttons," he said.

"Here, let me help." Applejack grabbed the spare pig suit and pushed the old Shire into the rear of the stable "There's no time to waste, we'll just have to put your pig disguise over your goat suit for now."

Willow watched as Miss Trudy opened the stable door, which was unusual, as she'd never seen her do it before, because door opening was Mr Neville's job. "Ooh you're adorable," she cooed, seeing the pink pig waiting inside. "Hello piggy."

Outside an engine died and a voice called, "Hello."

"Over here in the old stable," shouted Miss Trudy, scattering fresh straw across the floor. A figure blocked out the light in the open doorway and by its silhouette, Willow guessed it was the vet. "Where is he?"

"If by 'he' you're referring to my boyfriend, he's still in bed. He's been up all night."

"Lucky sod, I'd let you keep me up all night," the vet said tilting his head as he winked his eye: Because despite the many knockbacks he got, he still fancied his chances. "Get your mind out of the gutter," she told him with a sneer. "He's been up all night with the shits. I think he had a dodgy curry."

I see the pigs have arrived," Mr Clifford said as Applejack appeared through the door leading into the back of the stable. "Yes, they were already here when I arrived."

"Where's Chestnut?" whispered Willow to Applejack.

"He's in the back, don't worry he's changed into his pig disguise."

From the rear of the stable, a tearing sound grabbed everyone's attention, Miss Trudy began to walk towards the noise when Willow pushed Applejack forward blocking her way. Willow darted into the rear of the stable to find Chestnut standing with several long tears in his pig disguise. "I'm sorry Willow, I breathed out and the seams split."

"Quickly hide."

But it was too late, Miss Trudy had pushed passed Applejack and now stood looking at a goat draped in shredded pink fabric.

"What the fuck's going on?" called the vet, not known for his patience.

"There's a goat back here, and it's been buggering about with my fabric."

"Perhaps it wasn't wanted," the vet said poking his head around the door frame, before adding compassionately, "It does look like a knackered old beast. What will you do with it?"

"Get rid of it, we don't want any goats."

"I could take it off your hands if you like?" Willow saw Miss Trudy's eyes light up at the prospect of getting the problem sorted out quickly and without worrying her boyfriend. "Yes, won't cost you a penny, I can take it away right now."

"Okay, help yourself. I'd better get back. I'll no doubt have to stop off at the supermarket on the way for more bog-rolls and air freshener."

The two horse-pigs, and Chestnut, the horse-goat followed Miss Trudy out of the stable and watched as she left the field on Mr Neville's two-wheeled seat. After she had disappeared from view Mr Clifford fetched a rope from the brick box with the square glass eye, fixed it around Chestnut's thick neck and led him away.

Mr Clifford tied the old horse-goat to the fence and began to attach a two-wheeled tall crate to the back of his green box on wheels, giving the two horse-pigs a chance to talk to their friend.

"This is terrible Chestnut, what shall we do?" Applejack said.

"There's nothing we can do."

"But, there must be something?" sobbed Willow.

"I'm afraid not, we tried our best." Chestnut lowered his head towards Willow and whispered, "Thank you for everything you have done for us."

Mr Clifford came back and untied the rope, and leading Chestnut away, said, "You're such a fine goat and I know a Caribbean takeaway that makes a really good goat curry. They'll pay a handsome price for you." Because, as it's been said before: Mr Clifford, despite being a wealthy veterinarian, couldn't stop himself from being a money-grabbing sack of shit.

The two horse-pigs watched as Chestnut was led away, Willow had heard that in times of trouble, humans would often pray; but as she was a fucking horse and didn't know what praying was, she just hoped that somewhere there was a power that would see to it that her friend would come to no harm.

"Looks like it's just us two now," Applejack said.

Chapter Seven: Visitors

Applejack and Willow both thought that Mr Neville had done a good job of fixing up the stable. Willow particularly liked the flowers Miss Trudy had stencilled onto the new stable doors, although Mr Neville had asked her politely not to do it. The two horse-pigs really liked their refurbished home but couldn't understand why the humans kept calling it a sty.

Ever since the field had become his, Mr Neville had been making changes. He had put new fencing in and also taken the stile out, blocking the public right of way with a piece of meshed fencing. As far as he was concerned, no one was going to get into his field without permission.

The food had changed too, and now in addition to the dried feed, Mr Neville added lots of apples and carrots, much to the delight of the horse-pigs. One evening whilst patting Willow's flanks, he had commented that the extra food seemed to be doing the trick. She wasn't sure what he had meant by that, but she was becoming aware of her pig suit starting to feel uncomfortable. "Applejack," she asked one morning, "do my flanks look big in this?"

"Sorry, what do you mean?" he replied.

"Does your disguise feel tighter?"

"Now you come to mention it, yes it does rather."

"Mine too, and I fear the side stitching is beginning to give way."

"I hope not, the last thing we want is the sight of a pony spilling out of a pig."

That morning, as rain pinged and ponged off the stable roof, the two horse-pigs tried to work out how long it had been since Chestnut had been taken away. Willow explained to her friend that being equine they didn't have any concept of time, much like a dog that never really knows how long it's been separated from its human owner. But despite this, and being a lateral thinking pony, she said "I think I may have found a way of working out how many days have passed since we said goodbye to our old friend."

"Have you? Chestnut was quite right; you are a clever pony."

"Maybe. I was thinking, we sleep at the end of every day, and I have counted that since Chestnut was taken away I've had thirty-eight sleeps."

"So how many human weeks is that?"

"I don't know, because I'm a fucking pony."

"So we're none the wiser then?"

"It would appear that way, so I'm not that clever after all." Willow dipped her eyes looked at the ground and took comfort from her friend who empathetically nuzzled her neck with his.

"Good morning my lovely porkers," said Mr Neville as he opened the doors to reveal the grey day outside. Willow grunted her welcome but refused to move from her bed, the thought of getting wet not too pleasing. "Come along fatties," Miss Trudy said popping her head around the door, "Time for a little run."

"Fatties!" squealed Willow. "I don't know how she has the nerve."

"Me neither. Just look at the size of her arse, if that was in a butcher's window, you'd need to do a month's worth of overtime before you could afford to buy it."

"Oh Applejack I don't know how you can say that word," winced Willow.

"What, arse?"

"No, butcher."

"Come along my lovelies," Mr Neville said. "Come see what I've got for you".

The two horse-pigs trotted out of their snug home and followed him to the food trough. "What's that?" Applejack whispered to Willow.

"I'm not sure."

"Come on you lucky porkers," said Mr Neville, "Tuck in."

"Tuck in?" Willow said to Applejack. "I think he wants us to eat it."

"What, eat this shit, where are the fresh apples and carrots?"

"What's wrong with the pigs?" said Miss Trudy as she joined her boyfriend at the feeding trough. "They don't seem to like the food."

"They'll eat it when they're hungry. It's probably just because it looks different to what they're used to."

"And can your friend Cher guarantee us more?"

"Of course," Miss Trudy said. "The residents never eat all that's put in front of them, it's a waste if you ask me."

"Well, their loss is our gain."

"Or rather, the old folk's loss is our piggies' weight gain," said Miss Trudy, laughing at her own joke: Which quite frankly was a rather shit attempt at humour. She turned around, and before heading back down the field, said, "I'm off to clean out the sty, if you help me put down new straw, I'll maybe give you a blow job."

Willow watched as Mr Neville's face creased into a smile and before he'd had the chance to take Miss Trudy up on her offer, a voice at the gate called to him, "Excuse me, is this field yours?"

"No, it's the fucking Pope's," answered Mr Neville, turning around to see a man dressed in a suit and expensive-looking mackintosh standing at his gate.

"Well could you ask his holiness why he's blocked off the public right of way?" the officious looking man shouted back sarcastically.

"Because, he doesn't want hordes of people traipsing over his land, now if that's all, some of us have more pressing things to get on with."

The horse-pigs watched as Mr Neville turned his back on the man and strode off, unbuttoning his trouser front as he walked down the field in the direction of the stable.

A few minutes later, wet and still refusing to eat the food put out for them, the horse-pigs trudged through the mud-soaked grass towards their stable. Hearing a funny moaning sound coming from inside, Applejack looked around the doorframe, withdrew his head and turned to Willow. "I think Mr Neville has a puncture."

"A puncture?"

"He must have, Miss Trudy's on her knees in front of him and it looks like she's blowing him back up."

"That's human's for you," said Willow. "Unreliable physiology."

The horse-pigs walked back up the field and took shelter beneath the big tree, its green leaves were now beginning to turn golden brown. "I'm so hungry," said Willow.

"Me too, I can't believe Mr Neville wants us to eat that left-over human slop."

"Maybe tomorrow we'll get our proper feed."

"Do you think Mr Neville will be fully inflated yet?" Willow looked away from her friend, and shuddered, "I can guarantee, he's fully inflated."

***

The following morning when the doors were opened, the horse-pigs saw that the rain had gone away leaving behind a soggy field. Applejack stepped outside and shivered as the cold ran up his leg. Willow peered out over her friend's shoulder, "Looks nasty out there," she said.

"It is, but there's something much worse."

"What?"

"That." Willow looked over to see Mr Neville tipping a bucket of mixed kitchen waste into their food trough. "Come along fatties," chirped Miss Trudy.

"Do you know, one of these days she'll get one of my rear hooves in that fat arse of hers," said Applejack. Willow laughed and the horse-pigs walked over to the trough, sniffed at the mess of mixed swill and walked away again. "Do you know something," Willow said, resting her chin on the fence as she looked over at the motorway. "It's not so much fun watching the boxes on wheels now that the bumpy hole has gone."

Later that afternoon, Willow was standing watching Mr Neville, who was giving the gate a fresh coat of paint when a box on wheels pulled up. Out of it emerged a stern looking woman, holding what looked like a board with a clip attached to the top and under the clip was an envelope. "Excuse me, are you Mr O'Leary?" the woman said, with a voice that Willow thought was shrill and unpleasant. "Who wants to know?" Mr Neville replied, not bothering to look up from his gate painting. "The council, Mr O'Leary."

"Well, you're out of luck. I'm not Mr O'Leary and this place doesn't belong to him anymore."

"Well, it says here in my information that this land belongs to a Mr O'Leary."

"Well, it doesn't belong to him any longer. It's mine."

"Is everything okay?" Miss Trudy walked out of the brick box with the square glass eye to see what was going on at the gate. "It's just a nosey old crone from the council."

"You're a bit early love, it's not Halloween until the weekend," laughed Miss Trudy.

"Excuse me," the visitor said, "There's no need to be unpleasant."

"What does she want?"

"I'm not sure." Mr Neville put down his paintbrush and wiped his hands down the front of his shirt, streaking it with green paint. "So what do you want?"

"We've had a complaint. It says here that you've blocked off the public access to the land." She then looked down at the paper fixed to the board with a clip to reacquaint herself with the information there, before looking up again. "A member of the public contacted us, saying they had tried to use the footpath a week ago, but found it closed off."

"Oh yes, I remember," Miss Trudy said. "Some bloke came and tried to get into the field, I told him it was closed. He said he had the right of way and that he was a rambler. I told him, my aunt Violet often talks non-stop too, and she's got no chance of crossing the field either." Mr Neville started to laugh at his girlfriend's joke but stopped when the woman on the other side of the gate glared at him. "And how did this man take it?"

"I don't care, I told him to piss off."

"You told him to…"

"Yes, that's right," said Miss Trudy, joining her boyfriend at the gate. "Do you have a problem with that?" Willow noticed that the woman looked a little flustered when Miss Trudy spoke to her and she flicked through the pages attached to her board with a clip before regaining her composure. "Yesterday one of my colleagues came to talk to you and you told him that this field belonged to the pope."

"Yes, that's right."

"And why did you say that?"

"Because I had promised to nosh him off in the pigsty," Miss Trudy said laughing loudly, her response causing the visiting woman's cheeks to flush. "And we don't want strangers walking through the field disturbing the pigs." Mr Neville said. "Now if you've finished, I've got a gate to finish painting." The woman stepped forward and held out the envelope, Willow watched her flinch a little as Miss Trudy reached over to take it from her. "This is an instruction from the council. It gives you seven days to re-open the public right of way. Failure to do so will result in the council taking action against you. Good day."

Mr Neville and Miss Trudy watched as the woman returned to her box on wheels, and as she drove away they both blew a loud raspberry and stuck their fingers up in the air. Willow lowered her eyes and muttered to herself, "Common."

***

The next four days passed routinely, Mr Neville came to the field, let out the horse-pigs, refreshed their bedding and poured a bucket of kitchen waste into the feeding trough. The public right of way was re-instated, with Mr Neville removing the fencing he'd previously erected; this didn't stop him however from rubbing grease into the wooden step, saying "That'll show the field-plodding bastards."

As the days passed the horse-pigs became so hungry that they had begrudgingly began to eat the food put out for them, neither one enjoyed it and ate only enough to stave off the pains that gnawed at their insides. Their pig outfits began to feel more comfortable as the excess pounds started to drop off them and it was this weight loss that began to cause Mr Neville some concern. Because despite him being an uncouth dimwit, whose brains were in his boxers, he did care for the welfare of his livestock, and it was because of this concern that he had called the vet's surgery earlier.

Willow and Applejack were standing beneath the big tree, which that morning had begun to drop its leaves. They were watching as Miss Trudy used a knife to carve faces into fat orange vegetables when they saw Mr Clifford's green box on wheels arrive. He climbed out carrying a black case, and without looking up Miss Trudy called, "The twat's here."

Mr Clifford spotted the two bars of chocolate on the ground next to where she was sitting. "You'll spoil your figure eating those."

"Piss off, you knob jockey," Miss Trudy said, going back to scooping out pumpkin flesh with an old spoon.

"Oh dear, I think we're in trouble now," said Willow. "Mr Clifford has his case of pokey-proddy things."

"Pokey-proddy things?"

"Yes, the things he uses in his job. Once he starts poking and prodding he'll discover our secret. He'll find out that we're not real pigs."

"Bollocks," said Applejack. "Whatever shall we do?"

"I don't think there's anything we can do. Oh, my friend, your secret will be out as soon as he sticks one of his latex covered digits up your arse. I know it's a cliché but I'm rigid with fear."

"Willow, what's a cliché?"

"I don't know, because I'm a fucking pony."

They watched as Mr Clifford shook hands with Mr Neville, and behind his back, Miss Trudy formed a circle shape with her forefinger and thumb and moving it up and down she mouthed a word that Willow lip read as, anchor.

Just then the sound of another box on wheels arriving caused the three humans to turn around. The box stopped and a portly, white-haired man with oversized spectacles stepped out. "Fuck me," said Miss Trudy. "It's Hedwig,"

"Very original," said the man. "Are you the owner of this land?"

"No, he is," she said pointing to her boyfriend. "The chunky one that bears a striking resemblance to Coronation Street's Tyrone. The one that looks like a bosted clog's the local vet… or twat as I like to call him."

"Screw you," said Mr Clifford, and red-faced he stomped off through the gate and drove away. Because despite being a grown-up often reacted like a petulant child.

The bespectacled man stepped forward, offered his hand then withdrew it before Mr Neville could shake it, and said "My name is Mr Potter." Miss Trudy shrieked with laughter before saying, "Ha! Potter."

"How original," the man said giving Miss Trudy a look that did little to disguise his disgust. "I'm here about your pigs." Still shrieking with laughter Miss Trudy said, "Oh shit, I've just done a little wee. I'm going to have to sponge my gusset now."

"What about my pigs?" said Mr Neville, watching as his visitor sloshed his Wellington boots in the old washing-up bowl of disinfectant by the gate. The man looked over in the direction of the big tree and seeing the two horse-pigs said, "They're very odd-looking pigs."

"And when did you last take a look in the mirror?" sniped Miss Trudy, squatting as she used a tissue to pat at the crotch of her leggings. The man ignored her and turned to Mr Neville, "How long have these pigs been here?"

"What's it to you, it's none of your business?"

"It's very much my business, you see I'm here from the Department of Environment, Food and Rural Affairs. I'm *DEFRA*."

The horse-pigs by this time had sidled up to see what was happening and Applejack turned to his friend and said, "What did he say?"

"He said, he's Deborah," said Willow.

"Odd name for a man-human."

Trudy balled the tissue she'd been using and after sniffing it she dropped it into the disinfectant bowl. "You're too late mate, we've re-opened the public footpath."

"I'm not concerned about public rights of way, just the pigs."

"They're well looked after," blurted out Mr Neville.

"I don't doubt they are, but there are a few issues we have with your pigs. First, there appears to be no electric fence around the land?"

"That's right," Miss Trudy said. "Bloody cruel, if you ask me."

"Madam, I am not asking you, so if you'd kindly desist from interrupting." Mr Potter stopped, took a deep breath and removed a small notebook from the inside of his topcoat. He consulted the notebook and pointed towards the food trough. "You are aware, are you not, that it is illegal to feed kitchen waste to pigs?

"I... I didn't know," stammered Mr Neville.

"Hey, there's nothing wrong with that food, we get it from Happy Acorns Retirement Village." The white-haired man tossed Miss Trudy a sidelong glance and Willow thought, here's a human who won't take any shit. "And finally," Mr Potter said, "There's no record of your CPH registration."

"CPH?" said Mr Neville.

"Yes, without a CPH number, it's illegal to keep pigs."

"So what are you saying?" asked Trudy.

"What I am saying is this," said Mr Potter handing Mr Neville an official looking piece of paper. "You have seven days to have these pigs removed from this land. One of my colleagues will contact you to arrange a licence to move the animals. Failure to comply will result in prosecution, not to mention a hefty fine."

"Oh bugger," Willow said.

"What does all that mean?" asked Applejack.

"It means Mr Neville will have to get rid of us."

"What animal shall we disguise ourselves as next?"

"None, I'm afraid, looks like the game is up."

As Mr Neville and Miss Trudy watched Mr Potter's box on wheels drive away, the two horse-pigs walked back to the big tree and looked at the orange Halloween lanterns lying in the grass.

Chapter Eight: A Good Idea

A few mornings later, the horse-pigs were delighted to see that Mr Neville was taking down the pumpkin heads that Miss Trudy had lined up along the window ledge several nights earlier. Willow had not only been a little scared of the eerie faces that distorted as the candles inside had flickered but had been concerned that a live flame in close proximity to straw could have been a potential fire risk.

Willow shuffled out of the stable and saw Applejack up at the feeding trough having his breakfast; the two friends were pleased that since the visit from the man named Deborah, their food had returned to normal.

It had been windy during the night and the big tree had lost most of its leaves, they fluttered around the field in the light breeze like golden fish out of water. Willow knew that the humans called this time of year autumn, and of all of the human seasons, this one was her favourite.

"Good morning Applejack, isn't it a lovely day?"

"It certainly is," he replied with a half-eaten carrot sticking out of the side of his mouth. "You can almost feel the trees getting ready to sleep."

"Yes, this time of year is special."

"I love the morning fog and the earthy smell in the air. It's a shame that we won't be here much longer to enjoy it."

"How long do you think we have left?" her friend said, now munching on a crisp fresh apple. "I don't know, but I'm sure it can't be too long."

The two horse-pigs turned as they heard the familiar off-tune whistling of Mr Neville, he was pushing his wheelbarrow up the field, and Willow noticed, that dropped inside were Miss Trudy's carved pumpkin heads. At the big tree, he lowered the barrow onto its braces and began to fill it with the fallen leaves. "I shall miss him," said Applejack as he watched the stocky man bending down to scoop up a pile of ochre-coloured leaves. "I shan't miss that," said Willow, as Mr Neville's bum crack slid out above his jeans.

As the morning passed by the horse-pigs watched the comings and goings on the motorway, while Mr Neville transferred the raked-up leaves and unwanted pumpkin heads to the compost heap behind the brick box with the square glass eye. Willow noticed Mr Neville had only stopped once, and that was to pour some of the steaming liquid he called 'tea', from a tartan tube into a mug.

Later that morning, Mr Neville and the horse-pigs were taking shelter from a light shower of rain, when they heard someone calling from outside. "Sounds like Miss Trudy," whispered Willow.

"Hello," she called again. "It's only me."

"I'm in here, polishing my helmet," called Mr Neville.

"I might have known you dirty sod, put it away, you'll frighten the pigs."

"No you daft cow," Neville said as Miss Trudy entered the stable. I'm buffing my crash helmet. But if you fancy giving my other little helmet a rub, I won't object."

"Don't you ever think of anything else?"
"No."

Miss Trudy put the paper parcel she was carrying down upon a bale of straw, and pulled back the hood of her coat, freeing a mess of dark curls fringed with straggly wet tresses. "I've brought us some fish and chips." Neville watched as Miss Trudy's sausage-shaped fingers opened the paper covered parcel, its sweltering contents spilling free. The scent of deep fried potato and malt vinegar filled the air, its wet aroma flowing through the stable like a lazy river. "Can you pass me that newspaper please?" she said pointing to the copy of the Express and Star that her boyfriend had laid his crash helmet on.

Taking it from him, she tore it deftly into two halves and proceeded to divide the chips into two piles, before topping them both with a crisp, golden batter covered fish.

"A man called about the pigs today," Mr Neville said taking the portion of food she offered him. "He said someone is coming to collect them in four days, I just had to sign some forms."

"It'll be sad to see the porkers go, but I guess it's for the best."

Miss Trudy sat on the straw bale, her lunch balanced upon her knees with vinegar seeping through the newspaper and staining her leggings beneath. Neville nodded his response as he plucked a hunk of white flesh from his fish, and dropped it into his mouth, which was now a greasy slash in his face.

"Just look at them," Applejack whispered to Willow. "They eat like bloody animals."

After polishing off the last few chips, Mr Neville screwed his newspaper into a ball, rubbed his stomach and belched. Miss Trudy began to fold up her now redundant newspaper when she stopped suddenly. An article had caught her eye and looking at the grease-stained newsprint she said, "Oh my goodness, when was this?"

"When was what?" said Mr Neville, picking at his teeth with a fingernail.

"This." She held up the newspaper so that he could read the headline. "Pensioner leaves false leg in taxi."

"Not that headline you daft sod, this one." She was shaking the newspaper and pointing quite aggressively to a by-line above a photograph of the arts centre in Walsall. Neville grabbed the newspaper from her, and then scowled, because Trudy had hidden the skin she had stripped off her fish within its pages, and now it was squashed between his fingers. "Buggery bollocks," he said looking at his fingers covered in the greasy sequins of fish scales.

"Well, what do you think?"

"I think my fingers are going to smell all day now."

"Forget about the fish skin you daft twat, look at the article about the arts centre."

"Theatre Company looks for new venue. What about it?" he said more confused than normal as he read the story heading aloud.

"It's an opportunity."

"An opportunity?"

"Look," she said taking the paper from him, "it says there's been a small fire at the Forest Arts Centre and they are no longer able to stage this year's Christmas pantomime." Miss Trudy put the newspaper down, wiped the chip fat from her hand down the outside of her leg and rummaged through her coat pockets. "Here it is," she said, holding up a piece of card. "I picked this up in the library a few months ago."

"What is it?"

"It's a flyer for an outdoor theatre production."

"Outdoor theatre?"

"Yes. Travelling theatre companies set up outside and the public pays to sit on the grass and watch the show. Why don't we offer the pantomime company this field to perform their show in?"

"I can't see anyone wanting to come to sit in a field in December. It'll be cold, not to mention the probability of getting a wet arse."

We could make this work," Miss Trudy said. "If we get a large tent, hire some heating and some seating, this could be a nice little windfall for us."

"Sounds like a stupid idea if you ask me," said Mr Neville as he picked up his crash helmet and walked out of the stable. "He lacks vision," she said, turning to the horse-pigs. Reaching out she slid her hand over Willow's shoulder, "I'll just have to convince him that this could be a good thing for us."

Willow snorted, happy little grunts of pleasure, Miss Trudy looked deep into the horse-pig's amber eyes and said, "It's funny, but you remind me of a friendly lion I once knew."

Chapter Nine: Pantomime

A few days later, Mr Neville and Miss Trudy had arrived as they usually did. They opened the stable and poured feed into the trough, but this day was different, they appeared to be very interested in the size of the field.

The two horse-pigs watched as they laid out a flat ribbon-like tape across the surface of the ground, Mr Neville looked closely at it and then wrote in a notebook. The tape, when released by Miss Trudy recoiled back into its holder rather like an electrified serpent.

"What do you think they are doing?" asked Applejack.

"They're taking measurements," said Willow.

"What are measurements?"

"They are the process of determining the ratio of a physical quantity, such as length, time, temperature and so on."

"So do you know how to measure things, Willow?"

"Of course I do. How do you think I made all the disguises?"

A fat white box on wheels arrived at the field and out of it climbed three men, Mr Neville walked over and the horse-pigs watched as he pointed to various parts of their field. One of the men; a round fellow with a beard the colour of copper wire took out a rolled up piece of paper and opening it showed Mr Neville what was written there. After much head nodding the humans all shook hands and the three men took out a large bundle from the back of their fat box on wheels.

"Come on piggies," Miss Trudy said as she shook a bucket in their direction. "I'll get the pigs put away so you can start work."

"You can't have pigs here at the same time as a big top," the bearded man said.

"They're going tomorrow afternoon." Mr Neville said. "How long will it take you to set things up?"

"About five hours," the man said. "Once the show tent is up, the flooring will go down, followed by the heaters and the raked seating. Once it's complete, you'd never guess you were in the middle of a field."

Inside their stable, the horse-pigs wondered what could be going on outside in the field, as the duration of the passing day was taken up with a large amount of drilling, hammering and of course swearing: Because you see, most human men are unable to participate in manual labour without using profane words.

As dusk descended upon the field and after Mr Neville had been to say goodnight and check that the stable was secure, everything went quiet. Willow and Applejack were drifting off to sleep when they heard muffled voices outside.

Willow opened one eye and saw a light flash between the crack where the new doors didn't quite meet when closed. She recognised the sound of the door opening stick being inserted into the lock and the sound of the bolt drawing back. "Oh, I'm so excited," a girlish voice said.

"Me too," another voice said. This voice had a pseudo-feminine, almost girlish sound, but Willow knew it belonged to a human man. "Now don't disturb them," said Miss Trudy as the door swung open.

The two horse-pigs lifted their heads to see three people peering into the gloomy interior of the stable. Miss Trudy stepped forward, the arrow of light from her torch cutting through the darkness. Willow was unhappy with the disruption and grunted her displeasure. "Hello piggies," whispered Miss Trudy, "These two people have come to see you."

"Are these the people who've come to take us away?" said Applejack to Willow, who just shrugged.

"They are actors and they've never seen pigs before."

"Oh they are so adorable," said the man-human, jumping up and down and clapping his hands like a demented sea lion. The girl-human squealed a high-pitched sound that made the wax in Applejack's ears crack and set Willow's teeth on edge. "Oh, I could just eat up the lovely piggle-iggles," she said.

"Me too, they're so scrummy-yummy," he said.

"Twat," Miss Trudy said under her breath, coughing the word into her fist.

"Sorry, did you say something?"

"It's the straw," Miss Trudy lied. "Makes me cough." And raising her fist to her mouth again, she coughed, "Ball bag."

"It's a pity they'll be going tomorrow." The girl-human said.

"They have to, we can't stage the pantomime with the pigs here."

"Shame, I'd have loved seeing them every day."

"Can't be helped," Miss Trudy said to the man-human. "Do you know what time the company arrive tomorrow?"

"The trailers with the costume and set will get here just before breakfast, the cast should get here a little after ten. It's so exciting, to think we'll have an open-air pantomime in the field. It's going to be great fun. The company's very grateful that you came to its aid."

"We're just glad we could help. Come on, we need to let these pigs get some sleep, they've got a long day ahead of them."

Willow and Applejack watched as the stable door closed and the bolt was pulled across again, neither one speaking until they were sure the humans had walked far enough away.

"So that's what's happening," said Willow. "A pantomime."

"Pantomime?" said Applejack.

"Yes. It's a theatrical production, usually performed around Christmas and New Year, and made up of music, comedy, buffoonery, sexual innuendo and of course cross-dressing."

"Have you ever seen a pantomime?"

"Of course not. Don't be stupid, I'm a fucking pony."

***

The next morning, outside the stable, again much noise could be heard. People were shouting instructions and the mechanical sounds of boxes on wheels could be heard as gravel crunched beneath their wheels. The two horse-pigs wished they could see what was going on outside, but no one had been yet to open their stable door.

"The loose planks," Willow said, and Applejack lifted them so that they could both see what was happening. They watched as Miss Trudy poured mugs of hot steaming liquid from a big round metal drum sitting on a table that stood beneath a green-striped garden gazebo that Willow assumed was a designated refreshment area. She spotted the feminine-voiced man from the previous evening's visit and after learning his name by lip-reading she told Applejack it was Mr Michael.

At the top of the field a large box on many wheels, similar to the kind Willow had often watched trundling along the motorway was growling, its bottom was sending out puffs of smoke as it stood shuddering. A long box with many square glass eyes along its sides, was standing parallel to the hedge that bordered the field and there was a small set of steps leading up to the open double doors at its rear, on one of the doors was taped a sign. A printed list.

Mr Neville arrived on his two-wheeled seat, just as the box with many wheels was being reversed alongside the striped gazebo. "What's that for?" he called from the gate.

"Set's in this one," said a skinny man, who despite the cold was only wearing a pair of shorts and a vest. "Costumes are in the old coach."

Mr Neville opened the stable to let the horse-pigs out into the field. He called inside without taking his eyes off the activity at the top of his field. "There's food in the manger, and please try not to get under anyone's feet."

"Come on everyone," bellowed Miss Trudy. "Come grab a mug of something hot."

Soon the refreshment area was packed with humans blowing into steaming mugs and grabbing at biscuits from the tin that was open on the table. "Mr Neville looks nervous," said Willow. As the horse-pigs wandered over to take a closer look at what was going on. "He's standing at the edge of the human group, drowning a digestive."

"Oh look, Mr Michael has gone over to speak to him. I wonder if they are talking about us leaving today." Willow wandered over and pretended to be interested in a discarded Kit-Kat wrapper nearby. "And what part are you playing?" said Mr Neville.

"I'm Grizzabelle, one of Cinderella's sisters."

"Oh, an ugly sister then?"

"Well, yes, but I'm the sexy one," said Mr Michael pinching Mr Neville's cheek, making him flush pink. "Maybe when we have some free time, you could show me around town?"

"I… err… need to… to be somewhere," spluttered Mr Neville, turning quickly and sloping off in the direction of the brick box with the square glass eye. He hadn't gone far when the skinny man in the shorts and vest called to him. "What are those pigs doing out?"

"They'll be no bother."

"Look mate, we can't have pigs wandering around. Health and safety and the like, you'll have to put them away."

Mr Neville walked back and began to usher Willow and Applejack back down the field towards their stable. Willow turned and saw Mr Michael had left the group, he was now standing at the bottom of the field, looking over the fence at the M6. As she trotted inside the stable she saw him pull his jacket around his body to conserve warmth and begin to walk back.

Mr Neville scattered some fresh bedding into the stalls and sat upon a straw bale. Willow had seen the look now hanging from his face many times before, knowing that he felt uncomfortable around so many strangers.

A shadow entered the stable, crawling across the floor silently, "I bet it's warm in here," a voice said.

Turning Mr Neville saw Mr Michael standing in the doorway. "Oh… I mean, hello. What are you doing down here?"

"Just needed to stretch my legs," said Mr Michael, smiling broadly as he spoke. Mr Neville looked away, "I need to lock the stable."

"Don't let me stop you."

Willow watched as Mr Neville pulled one of the doors closed and bent down to slide the downward bolt into its recess in the concrete floor. He twisted and turned the bolt which refused to move easily. Willow observed as looked behind himself at Mr Michael and then pulled his jeans up to cover his arse crack. "It's a bit stiff," he said, as the metal protested. "You don't say. Can I help in any way?" Willow saw Mr Neville half close his eyes and beads of sweat squeezed themselves out onto his forehead as Mr Michael placed his hand on top of his. "Oh yes, it is rather stiff, isn't it? I think it needs a little grease, there's nothing like a bit of lube to ease something into a tight spot." Willow wondered why Mr Neville's face had suddenly gone from pink to puce.

Quickly, Mr Neville stood up and stepped away before looking down to see Mr Michael was still holding his hand. "You've got such big strong hands."

"I have... um... have I?"

"Oh yes, such manly hands, the hands of a worker, not like mine, here feel how soft they are."

"I'd rather not." Mr Neville pulled his hand away and pressing himself against the walls of the stable he slid away. Mr Michael lifted his boot and placed it on top of the stiff bolt and with one swift push it moved downwards and into its recess. "See you piggies." And as he left he closed the stable door behind him.

"I don't want to be in here," said Applejack. "How are we supposed to know what's going on out there, if we're locked in here?"

"We'll have to peep through the loose planks again." So the two horse-pigs entered the rear of the stable and slid them aside. New humans were now unloading giant flat canvases from the large box on many wheels; canvases with painted scenes upon them. One was a flower-strewn meadow with a castle in the distance, another was a grey bleak wall with stubby candles burning in bronze-coloured sconces. Outside the long box with many square glass eyes, humans were standing in a line, and every now and then, one or two would walk up the steps and disappear behind its doors. "I wonder what's going on," said Applejack.

"There's only one way to find out," said Willow. "Follow me."

The two horse-pigs pushed themselves through the gap in the stable wall and crept along the perimeter of the field, keeping their bodies flush with the hedge as they walked. When they reached the long box with many square glass eyes they squeezed between it and the fence.

Willow spotted a gap between the door and the side of the box and squinting, she looked inside. Humans were coming to undress and try on different items of clothing, before leaving.

"What's happening?" whispered Applejack.

"The humans are trying on their costumes."

"Costumes, what are costumes?"

"The humans wear them so that they can make-believe they are different people when they perform in the pantomime. It's pretty much the same as how we've been using our disguises, to pretend to be different animals."

"If we could have two of those disguises, we could maybe stay in the field, instead of leaving later."

"Applejack, you wonderful, clever thing," Willow said, placing a kiss on his forehead, making him blush. "That's exactly what we'll do, when the humans have gone, we'll find ourselves something to wear from their disguise room."

As the minutes ticked away, the line of people dwindled until there was no one left at the small set of steps. A rotund man with a florid complexion and a scarf around his neck walked over to the long box with many square glass eyes and popping his head inside said, "Is that all the cast done?"

"Yes," a voice inside replied. "Everyone sorted, that is until the director chooses who wears this one." Willow imagined that the voice inside was showing the round man a costume he wasn't keen on, as he responded by saying, "They won't get me in that sodding thing, this year." The voice inside laughed, and Miss Trudy yelled across the field that it was lunchtime.

The horse-pigs watched as all the humans left the field, Applejack raised himself onto his back legs and looking over the fence he saw them walking towards the place Mr Neville had often called, the pub. "Are they gone?" Willow asked.

"Yes."

"Quickly, there's no time to waste."

Once inside the horses stripped off their pig disguises and searched for anything that they thought would fit them. Applejack tried to squeeze his flanks into a medieval peasant costume, while Willow tried on a kimono and turban. "It's no good, there's nothing here that's suitable," Applejack said as he tried on a ball gown and gemstone tiara. "Look," said Willow pointing to a suit draped over a large wooden trunk. "This is perfect."

"What is it?" said Applejack nudging the fabric with his nose.

"Isn't it obvious?" said Willow. "It's a horse disguise."

"What are you saying: that we as horses should, disguise ourselves, as horses?"

"Not exactly horses, plural, but just one horse."

"How?"

"Look this is a costume that's designed for two humans to wear at the same time."

Willow could see her friend was about to ask another question when outside the humans could be heard coming back into the field. The horses quickly scrambled into the horse suit; Willow at the front with Applejack taking the rear half.

From inside the costume, the horses heard the voice from earlier enter the room, "What's going on here?" The horse-pantomime-horse turned around and the voice laughed, "I see that the last costume has been allocated, so glad it fits. Now if you don't mind, get out of my costume department, dress rehearsal has been called for three-thirty."

The horse-pantomime-horse left the long box with many square glass eyes just as Mr Neville was walking up the field shaking his head. "I'm sorry, I can't help you," he told a man at the gate who Willow had never seen before. "The pigs are no longer here; someone must have collected them while we were at lunch." The man at the gate harrumphed and forced a piece of paper into Mr Neville's hand before turning on the heel of his Wellington boot and walking away.

"We did it," Willow said, "We're safe."

Chapter Ten: The Last Mince Pie

Willow and Applejack were nervous when the rehearsal started. As neither of them had ever seen a show before and had no idea what happened during a dress rehearsal; let alone how to act. It turned out however that they needn't have worried. The afternoon was a jumble of stop-start scenes interrupted by the humans operating the lights and sound; this led to a few of the actors shouting out choice words and one incident of someone throwing what Willow overheard to be a 'paddy'.

The horse-pantomime-horse waited backstage and watched everything that was happening on the stage. Well to be honest it was Willow who watched as poor Applejack was playing the back end of the horse, so the only thing he could see was the inside of the costume and Willow's buttocks. They learned very quickly that they were in two scenes. One where two men pretending to be ugly women, and siblings of a pretty girl have a riding lesson, and another where they had to pull a small, overly ornate box on wheels containing the pretty sibling who was pretending to be called Cinderella.

The dress rehearsal lasted well into the night, and after the actors and stagehands had left, Willow and Applejack, who had been hiding behind the long box with many square glass eyes, made their way wearily to the stable, with Willow hoping that every day wouldn't last as long.

***

They managed to muddle through the first show, despite being called a stupid pair of tosspots for missing their first cue. Willow, who had made a mental note to find out what a tosspot is, was taken aback by the strangeness of being in a show. Nothing could have prepared her for the wave of noise that seemed to rush up onto the stage when the humans who were sitting watching laughed, sang or banged the palms of their hands together. Applejack had asked her why the humans made cow noises when the two ugly sisters came onto the stage, and she had, during a quiet moment backstage whispered to him that they were not mooing but booing. This explanation in itself didn't answer her friend's question, and if anything she felt it had confused him further.

Willow very much liked being in the glamorous business of show, as she'd called it, but Applejack thought it wasn't all it was cracked up to be, saying that spending two hours staring up a horse's arse was not his idea of a glamorous profession.

Each day they performed two shows, one which they'd heard an actor call the matinee and the other that another actor had referred to, as the one that cuts into drinking time at the pub.

***

One evening, after the show, the actors packed away their things and left the field quicker than they usually did, with most dashing off in their boxes on wheels to an assortment of greetings, and promises not to be late back after the festivities.

Inside the stable Willow shuffled and stretched on her straw bed, getting comfortable, "We've got a whole day off tomorrow," she said

"Have we, why?"

"Because it's December the twenty-fifth."

"Is that an important day?"

"Yes, it's what the humans call Christmas Day. A day that they celebrate by getting into debt, buying and giving presents to other humans that they don't speak to for the rest of the year."

"Sounds very silly if you ask me," said Applejack yawning, "but, I think I'm going to quite enjoy having a day off though."

"Me too," said Willow, also yawning. And within minutes the stable was filled with the comfortable sound of sleep.

Christmas morning arrived in the field, the ground outside the stable door twinkled like someone had tossed a handful of faceted gemstones across its surface. Willow cautiously stepped outside, her breath steaming as she filled her lungs with wintery air. Looking around, the pony saw that no one was around, the performance tent and long boxes stood discarded and empty. Willow thought they looked creepy standing so silent after the clamour that had surrounded them previously.

"Morning," Applejack said.

"Morning," said Willow. "It's so nice being in the field and not wearing a disguise."

"Is it safe?"

"I think so. But just for today."

"Will someone be coming to feed us?"

"No. Don't forget, no one knows we're here."

Free from the pantomime costume, the two horses trotted and cantered around their field, they chased after each other and occasionally whinnied. Applejack gave a loud snort that sent a rabbit scurrying for cover, making Willow laugh. Breathing heavily from their endeavours they came to rest beside the fence and stood looking over the silent motorway.

"Close your eyes," said Applejack. Willow looked puzzled, but her friend just nodded his head, so she closed her eyes and waited. "You can open them now."

Willow opened her eyes to see him nudging a red apple across the ground towards her. "Happy Christmas, Willow."

"Is that for me?" she asked.

"Yes, it's a present from me to you."

"Oh, Applejack, thank you. No one has ever given me a present before. I'm so sorry, I don't have one for you."

"You've given me enough already."

"I don't understand?"

"The disguises you've made for us all have proved what a good friend you are." Willow blushed and then bit the apple into two halves and handed one half to her friend.

Later that day as they sat in the stable the conversation centred around what they thought the humans would be doing on their Christmas day. They also talked about their lost friends; both of them shedding a tear as they wondered where they were now, hoping they were all safe.

***

The following day the actors returned and the pantomime resumed and the horse-pantomime-horse performed two shows to humans who laughed, cheered and sang along. After the performance, the fear they had experienced every night since the pantomime had begun, came again. Worried that they'd be asked to take off the horse suit, Willow and Applejack drifted away from the cast, to hide until the field was free of humans. This evening as the props and costumes were being put away one of the actors was overheard saying, "Only ten more shows."

Later, in their stable Willow told Applejack what she had heard. "Does that mean we only have a few days left?"

"I'm not sure," said Willow.

"How will we know when it's the last show?"

"We'll have to count. You do know how to count don't you?"

"No, because I'm a fucking horse."

"Then I know what will help you," said Willow. "Mince pies."

"Mince pies?"

"Yes, the actors have a plate of them, ten in total that they use in a counting routine, I'll sneak out and see if they are still backstage."

Willow slipped out of the horse costume and nervously she left the stable through the loose planks in the rear and staying close to the hedge she crept towards the performance tent. At the entrance to the tent sat Mr Neville, he was asleep and snoring. Mr Neville was acting as the security guard; being too tight to employ a real one.

Willow saw that the tent was still open and being careful not to disturb Mr Neville, the pony crept inside. With the lights off it was dark backstage, but Willow had got used to walking around the unlit space during the shows.

She stepped around the overly ornate box on wheels, standing idle until the next show, and edged past the table that the actors put their props on, almost knocking over the bucket of confetti that the human playing Buttons used in a throwing water over the audience joke, that he never quite got right.

"There it is," Willow said seeing the tray of pies beside the stage manager's chair. She squeezed between the chair and tent pole and as she did this, her rump accidentally brushed against the button on the stage manager's microphone, turning it on. The pony stretched forward and closing her mouth around the edge of the tray she lifted it from the table.

Shuffling backwards her flanks rubbed across the top of the microphone, sending a rasping sound into the still of the evening.

At the front entrance disturbed by the sound, Mr Neville awoke, stretched and listened wide-eyed as the sound of something slithering across the floor echoed through the tent.

Backstage Willow was having trouble balancing the tray, it tilted forward and the taste of metal made her teeth buzz. She snorted and puffed as she wriggled backwards, the microphone picking up the sounds.

As she entered the auditorium, Willow saw Mr Neville switch on his torch and she ducked down as its yellow beam arced across the raked seating. "Hello, is anyone there?" Willow held her breath, fearful of being caught. Mr Neville began to walk along the row of seats that hid the pony; he was just a few footsteps away when a draught blew some of the icing sugar off the mince pies onto Willow. She carefully placed the tray on the ground and shook the sugar away from her nose, but as she did this she inhaled and the white powder tickled, making her want to sneeze. The pony wrestled with the urge to sneeze until it was impossible and let out a snort that reverberated through the tent, making, Mr Neville jump, fart and then run outside into the darkness of the open field.

Willow picked up the tray and after checking that it was safe to leave the tent she trotted back to the stable. Applejack was baffled as he watched his friend line up the mince pies on the empty tack shelf. "These will help you to count how many shows we have left," she said. "I've put ten pies here and after each show, you can come back and eat one of them. That way you'll know how many shows we have left to perform."

"What a brilliant…" Outside lights lit up the field, preventing Applejack from finishing his sentence, the two friends peeked through the loose planks and saw the performance tent was illuminated and that humans were milling around with torches, everyone appeared to be looking for something. For several minutes voices were raised before the lights inside the tent were extinguished, and the horses heard a man say, "That chubby bloke that owns the field, said he thinks the tent's haunted."

"Haunted," said Applejack.

"Ghosts," wailed Willow. Both of the horses' ears flattened in fear, and that night they slept together in one stall.

***

The morning of the last mince pie eventually arrived, and the horses climbed into their costume for the final performance. "What will happen after the pantomime ends?" said Applejack sadly, as he was whispering into her backside, Willow didn't hear him. The horse-pantomime-horse walked over to the backstage area and joined the actors for the final show.

The audience was in good form, and the actors played tricks on each other. Applejack was pleased to have finished performing in the horse riding scene, as it had felt that as the weeks had passed by the actor who sat on his back had got heavier.

The curtain fell for the last time, and after several encores, there was lots of hugging, kissing and general back-slapping backstage by the actors. As the crew began to strike the set, the horse-pantomime-horse heard humans make promises of staying in touch and as the costumes were delivered to a large wicker hamper and dropped into it, some even talked about liking posts on Instagram and looking for each other on a thing called Facebook. A hand slapped Applejack's backside, and a voice said, "Come on you two, let's have that costume for the cleaners." Willow snorted, nodding her head, the voice laughed. "Come on guys, it's time to come out of character."

As usual Willow and Applejack slipped away, they undressed out of the costume and left it on the steps of the long box with many square glass eyes. "Oh dear," said Willow.

"What's wrong?" Applejack asked.

"The humans who've come to take the tent down have parked their fat white box on wheels beside the stable and blocked the loose planks, we won't be able to sneak in without being seen. We'll be in serious trouble if Mr Neville catches us."

"Relax, I heard him say he was taking Miss Trudy home straight after the show. All we need to do is lie low until everyone has left."

"But we can't stay here, as soon as they move the long box with many square glass eyes, they'll find us hiding."

"I have an idea," said Applejack. "The hole in the hedge that you took Joshua-James through, we could squeeze through and hide in the next field."

"We'll never make it across to the other side of our field without being seen."

"I know, why don't I run out and get the humans' attention and then you can run across the field, they won't see you if they're too busy chasing after me."

"But you can't do that, what about you?"

"The gate is bound to be open so that the long boxes can pass through. I'll just run straight through it, and then meet you in the next field."

"I'm not sure. It sounds dangerous," said Willow.

The sound of someone securing the doors of the long box that had been the costume department signalled that the humans were almost ready to move out. Applejack said, "There's no time to lose." He let out a loud whinny and ran out into the field. Willow saw that the sight of a horse running up the field caused quite a commotion; someone shouted, "Where the fuck did that come from?" and another man screamed, "Run!" The urgency in his voice was evident, as he tried to escape the grey horse that was running straight towards him.

Willow used her friend's diversion to dash across the field and reach the gap in the hedge. She squeezed through, the bare twigs scratching at her skin. She turned and saw that Applejack seemed to be enjoying himself; how grand he looked with his mane billowing behind him as he ran.

She watched as he stopped short of trampling one of the workers and reared up onto his back legs, before turning and running in the direction of the gate. "Oh no," said Willow, breathing in sharply when she saw that the gate was closed.

Applejack cried out as he skidded to a halt. There was no way he could jump over it, the gravel on the other side would make landing tricky. He turned around, ready to make a dash for the hole in the hedge opposite.

A familiar sound appeared in the lane leading to the field, and Willow could see that it was Mr Neville returning on his two-wheeled seat, her eyes reached out and connected with Applejack's and as they stared at each other briefly, she willed him to think of a way to save himself. Applejack turned, and as if he'd heard her thoughts he rushed back towards the long box on many wheels and clambered inside. "NO!" mouthed Willow, no sound escaping as she spoke.

"What's going on here?" Mr Neville called seeing the empty field. "Where is everyone?" As the tent spat out the frightened humans, Mr Michael walked over and Willow heard him say, "There was a horse, a big grey, crazy fucking horse."

"Well there's no horse now," Mr Neville said: To be frank, he had grown tired of the actors and crew and couldn't wait to see them gone. "Come along, let's get this field cleared?"

From the other side of the fence, Willow waited patiently as the performance tent was taken down and neatly packed into the fat white box on wheels. Fearing that Applejack would be discovered as the sound system was dismantled and loaded into the long box on many wheels, she held her breath.

Two large L-shaped boxes on wheels arrived at the field, the first thundered through the gate, its engine growling and its great eyes glaring – white orbs of anger in the dusk. It stopped and then backed up to the long box with many square glass eyes. Willow heard the clanking of metal and then watched as it inched forward and turning in a semi-circular manner moved forward and out of the gate.

The doors to the long box on many wheels were closed and although the lack of light made it difficult to make out what was happening in any great detail, Willow watched as a tall, wiry man secured a metal tag around the locks.

Mr Neville shook hands with the wiry man and pressing herself into the hedge Willow heard them talking. "It's been an experience," Mr Neville said, "So is that it for another year?"

"No, this lot's needed for another show. We have to get the set and electrics down to Southampton, it'll be loaded onto a cargo ship next week and heading to Shanghai."

"Shanghai?"

"Yes, the company are performing over there. The containers will take about fifty-nine - sixty days to get there. There's another cast of actors and crew out there at the moment rehearsing the show." He whistled and waved to the other L-shaped box on wheels, its eyes opened, spilling brightness onto the trampled grass. Willow felt a lump form in her throat as it reversed up to and connected with the remaining long box. "Oh well, better get off," the wiry man said, before striding over towards the L-shaped box and after opening a door high in its side, he climbed inside.

As it began to leave, Willow thought she could hear Applejack neighing inside, and she became worried that he'd be crushed by moving canvases as the huge box twisted out of the gate and through the bend in the lane. Again she thought she could hear her friend, but as it disappeared into the night the L-shaped box on wheels honked, drowning out the grey horse's cries.

Willow watched as Mr Neville closed the gate and looked out over the now empty field, he straddled the two-wheeled seat and making it growl he rode away.

When she felt it was safe to come out of hiding, Willow pushed her way through the gap in the hedge, this time, not caring for the brittle twigs that grazed her skin. With her ears flattened, and her eyes leaking fat blobs of salty water down her face, she walked back to the stable, squeezed between the loose planks and spent the night looking at the last mince pie sitting on the tack shelf.

Chapter Eleven: Happy New Year

Many days passed before Willow stepped outside of the stable again. Every waking hour had been filled with thoughts of Applejack. The previous evening she had been disturbed by flashing lights; crackling fountains of stars ejaculating into the night sky.

The screams and explosions had kept her awake until the early hours, and as dawn had broken, she had managed to sleep, albeit fitfully, dreaming that her friend had been discovered and rescued from the long box on many wheels.

A little scared, Willow ventured outside. Worried about being discovered, she blinked in the bright sunshine and her stomach groaned. Mr Neville hadn't been to the field since the theatre company had left, and she had been so hungry that she'd eventually eaten the last mince pie. In the next field, she could see the thick clumps of grass that had grown undisturbed. Lush and green, and free from the trampling feet of humans; those feet that had turned her field into a threadbare muddy patch of earth.

Willow was nibbling at a pitiful patch of weeds when she heard Mr Neville's voice, looking up she saw him pushing his two-wheeled seat along the lane, his talking oblong pressed against the side of his head.

Quickly she darted to the edge of the field and tucked herself as close to the hedge as she could, hoping he wouldn't spot her. But the nude branches did little to conceal the sand-coloured pony. "Goodness me," said Mr Neville. "What are you doing here?" He leant his two-wheeled seat against the fence and climbed over the stile, clucking his tongue as he lifted his leg over the wooden bar. "Come on girl."

The pony trotted over to Mr Neville and enjoyed the horse and human contact as his hand caressed her nose, "I don't know how you got here old girl, but it looks like you could do with something to eat." Willow tossed her mane and walked behind him as headed towards the brick box with the square glass eye. He reached into his pocket and took out a bunch of door opening sticks. "I think there are some horse nuts inside, and maybe a little hay left over.

Willow nibbled at the sweet-tasting hay and horse nuts, her hunger fading with each mouthful. As she watched Mr Neville fill the drinking trough with fresh water she wondered if her discovery would mean that everything could go back to how it was, back to the time before disguises. Perhaps Mr Neville would bring in some other horses to keep her company, she thought, or possibly he could find her old friends? Life would be perfect then.

Sadly Willow's optimism was short-lived. She looked up from her breakfast to see a box on wheels arrive, and a man began to fix a familiar looking sign to the fence post beside the gate. Willow recognised the sign as the same one that Mr O'Leary had used before Mr Neville had owned the field. So once again, Willow knew that her home was up for sale.

The man who had nailed the sign to the post was looking at Mr Neville's two-wheeled seat, particularly the front black ring, which was deflated. "What happened?"

"I hit a bloody hole on the motorway, looks like the front wheel will need replacing."

"I'd get onto the highways agency if I was you. Make the bastards pay."

"I will. They only repaired the damned thing a few months back."

"It'll be the frost that's opened it up again."

Realising that the two humans were talking about the bumpy hole, Willow trotted down the field to take a look. Popping her head over the fence she saw the boxes on wheels manoeuvring around the hole in the motorway, as they had done before. She smiled as occasionally one would drop into the hole, its body dipping down then lurching back up. I guess the humans will come along with their upside-down cones and fill it in again soon, she thought.

Willow turned around as Mr Neville approached her, she saw that the sign fixing human had gone, and beside the gate now stood a fat orange box on wheels with a man fixing the two-wheeled seat. "I'll have to make sure you're okay. I'll give the vet a call." Upon hearing the V word, the word that meant Mr Clifford, Willow shook her head and whinnied. "Before I do that though, I'd better go and open the stable doors and make sure you've enough straw to sleep on.

As Mr Neville worked inside the stable, Willow heard a voice call out, a voice so small that the words couldn't be distinguished. She turned and looked up the field she saw a small human-girl standing outside the gate. The girl called again and then began clucking her tongue. Willow clicked her back hooves together and cantered towards the gate, as she approached she saw the girl was holding out something round and white with a hole in its middle. "Hello pony, would you like one of these?" she said. Willow stopped, nodded and gently took the white ring from the girl. The explosion of mint flooded the pony's mouth; this was quite unlike anything she had ever tasted before and she liked it, in fact, she liked it very much.

"What do we have here?" said a human-man coming from behind a tree. What is it with trees, thought Willow that men feel the need to pee up them? I guess I'll never know because I'm a fucking pony. "It's a pretty pony," the girl replied. "I gave her my mint, ponies like mints."

The sand-coloured pony quite liked being called pretty; pretty pony, it sounded much nicer than fucking pony. Her ears moved forward to show just how pleased she was. The girl offered her another mint and smiling; her first smile since losing Applejack, she took the offered sweet.

Mr Neville appeared from inside the stable and seeing the two people at the gate he walked over to them. "Nice little pony," the man said. "Is it yours?"

"Yes, she is, her name's Willow."

"Ooh, what a lovely name," said the girl.

"I see you're selling the field."

"Yes, I'm moving, away so won't be around to look after it."

"Really," the man said. "You moving far?

"Only Wolverhampton, my girlfriend thinks it's time I moved in. Sadly though, it'll be too far for me to travel from every day. You're not interested in a field are you?"

"Thank you, but, no. We've already got a paddock at home." A paddock thought Willow, how lovely would it be to have your own paddock. "So what'll happen to the pony?"

"I'll have to find a new home for her."

"Well," said the man, "My daughter seems quite taken with her. If you decide to sell I might be interested."

"Ooh Daddy, please, please can I have the pretty pony?"

Hearing this, Willow thought that if she had fingers like the humans had, she might have crossed them. She stopped herself from crossing her hooves. Crossed hooves she thought would just make her look twisted and nobody would want to buy a twisted pony.

"It's not up to me," the man said. "This gentleman here owns the horse." Upon hearing this Mr Neville puffed out his chest, no one had called him a gentleman before. "I think we could come to some arrangement."

Willow watched the two men do the strange holding hands and moving up and down thing that she'd seen many times before. Knowing that the handshaking meant that a decision had been made, she smiled as the man said, "You don't mind if we ask for a health check first?"

"No, I'll get my vet to sort one out for you." The man turned to the girl and said, "Looks like the pony will be yours after all darling, happy new year."

***

"So you've managed to sell the old nag," Mr Clifford said the next day when he visited the field. "Yes, just as long as she's got no health problems. The new owners want to collect her tomorrow."

"Okay, I'll give her the once over, but it'll cost you."

Willow was tethered to the gate post and stood there as Mr Clifford the vet poked and prodded at her. He looked at her teeth and inside her ears, and after lifting her tail made her squirm as he plunged his fingers where Willow would have preferred him not to. Mr Clifford lifted her front hooves one by one and picked at them with a sharp thing that made her wince. "The best place for you is the glue factory," he laughed as he now picked up one of Willow's back legs and scraped at the underside of her hoof.

"How is it going?" asked Miss Trudy walking over and stroking Willow's nose. "It's lovely to see you again old girl."

"Almost finished," said Mr Clifford who was looking at Miss Trudy's tummy, which seemed to have grown bigger over the past weeks. "Bloody hell, you've put some weight on."

"Do you know, for a so-called professional you really are a stupid man. I'm pregnant, you daft bastard."

"I didn't think your fella had it in him."

"Just sort out the pony, you pathetic excuse for a man and then, you can fuck right off."

"I'd rather sort you out," laughed the vet.

Willow saw the vile man grab at his crotch and pull a face and purse his lips, which made them look like two red slugs being sucked from beneath the soil. "Come on, be honest you know you'd like a bit of this."

"In your dreams, dickhead, just look over the pony."

"Okay, I'll sort out your old nag." Old nag thought Willow, I'll show you. She lifted her left back hoof and with as much force as she could muster, she swung it backwards, hitting the vet squarely in the crotch. It has to be said that, the noise that comes from a veterinarian with crushed testicles isn't a pleasant one.

Mr Neville came running to see what all of the hullabaloo was and found his girlfriend laughing like an asthmatic warthog that had run out of Ventolin. "Are you okay?" he asked the doubled-over vet.

"Of course not, you dim-witted idiot."

"That was classic, well-done Willow," laughed Miss Trudy.

"You'll get my bill in the morning," said Mr Clifford, trying his best to stomp off, but only managing to hobble. "Oh by the way," Mr Neville called.

"What?"

"Piss off, you money-grabbing bastard."

***

The next day, Willow waited impatiently at the gate for her new owners to come to collect her. Mr Neville had arrived at the field early and had given her a good grooming. Her coat shone in the early morning sunshine and Miss Trudy had plaited her mane, fixing it with a yellow ribbon.

"Looks like they're here," Mr Neville said as the sound of a box on wheels on could be heard coming down the lane. Willow's heart skipped as it came into view, coming to rest just outside the gate. "Morning," said Miss Trudy as the man climbed out. "She's all ready for you." A squeal pierced the air and the girl from the day before ran towards the gate. Willow saw that the girl was happy and that her eyes were wide with excitement, she wondered if her own eyes told of the excitement she also felt.

"Did you get her health checked?"

"Yes, I telephoned this morning and the vet's report is ready. Would you like me to drive over to Bloxwich and fetch it for you?"

"I need to call into town, so I can collect it then. Would it be okay for me to leave the horsebox here?"

"No problem, we'll get Willow safely inside for when you return."

Willow watched the man walk back to his box on wheels and turn it around, he drove it backwards into the field and through the gate that Miss Trudy had just opened.

Once inside the gate, the man then disconnected the two-wheeled tall crate he had arrived with, before exiting into the lane again. What's happening, thought Willow, seeing the man leave, has the human changed his mind?

"Come along my beauty, let's get you all loaded up." Miss Trudy slipped a halter over Willow's head and led her up the ramp and into what she now knew was called a horsebox. "The nice man will be back for you in a few minutes." Willow allowed herself to be tethered and waited as Miss Trudy secured the rear bar, before taking the brush out of her pocket to give the pony's tail a final run through with its bristles. "I don't know why," she said, "But I feel like I have known you for ages." Willow smiled as Miss Trudy leaned over and kissed the top of her head.

As she waited patiently for her new owners to return, thoughts raced around the pony's head, and dreams of a bucolic existence faded in and out behind her eyes. Visions tumbled like numbered balls in a fortune-predicting machine. Dreams of trotting along with the small girl sat upon her back, of cantering in the sun and nibbling the heads off dandelions. Life looked like it was going to be perfect after all.

The purring engine signalled the return of the man and the girl, and from inside the box, Willow could hear the crunch of gears as her new owner's box on wheels reversed. "Okay, you can stop there." She heard Mr Neville shout. "Do you want me to fasten the trailer coupling?"

"Best let me do it," she heard the man say. "It's a bit temperamental."

Willow listened as outside the man tried to connect the horsebox. Bollocks, bollocks, bollocks." She heard him say.

"Is everything okay?" asked Mr Neville.

"I just pinched the skin between my forefinger and thumb. It's a bugger to get this coupling attached sometimes." The pony inside heard a loud click and the man said, "All done."

Mr Neville rapped on the side of the horsebox; his way of saying goodbye and Miss Trudy popped her head over the tailgate to blow the pony a final kiss. The box shuddered and slowly began to move away, the wheels dipped and rose on the uneven surface of the field before becoming more stable as it entered the lane. Looking through the slit of a window in front of her, Willow saw that they were now curving the bend and as the box carried her along. A breeze was sucked inside the box making her lashes flutter and tears prick at her eyes.

A few minutes later Willow felt the box slow then arc as if travelling around a sharp bend until she realised she was on the great grey path she had often looked at from the field. "I can't believe that I'm actually on the motorway," she told herself. "I'm on the M6."

Excited and with a heart full of hopefulness, she closed her eyes enjoying the ride. She tried to remember but couldn't think of a time when she'd ever felt like this before, only one thing before had made her feel this happy, and that was when Applejack had given her the red apple at Christmas.

Willow was enjoying the ride when suddenly the box dropped down, lurching to the left. It then sharply rose again, then began wobbling from side to side. "The bumpy hole," she said, as suddenly from outside a loud scraping sound could be heard. Looking through the window she saw her new owners moving at an odd angle, veering to the left whilst she carried on in a straight line. Sparks flashed up from the road surface and Willow realised that the two boxes on wheels had separated.

The horsebox began to slow and as it did it tilted to the left, righted itself then tilted again before falling. The metal trim screamed as it came into contact with the road and the horsebox wall began splintering as it slid across the hard surface of the motorway.

The fall had forced the air from her lungs and the pony lay tethered inside, fighting to breathe. She felt a little dizzy but was relieved that despite a sore shoulder she wasn't in any real pain.

Eventually, the box stopped skidding and came to a standstill. Outside Willow could hear the sound of metal coming into contact with metal, followed by the frantic calls of humans, she wondered if Mr Neville and Miss Trudy had been watching the motorway from the field and had seen what had happened.

An odd stillness hung in the air and her heart slowed to normal and her breathing returned. Looking through the window Willow could see the two square eyes of a long box on many wheels thundering towards her and taking a deep breath, the sand-coloured pony closed her eyes.

Chapter Twelve: Willow's Surprise

The sand-coloured pony whinnied and her eyes opened, wide and gazed into the gloom. She was cold and as the sweat on her body cooled she shivered. "Another one," she said, recalling the nightmare that had disturbed her sleep, "when will they end?"

Many weeks had passed since the incident on the motorway and Willow had escaped serious injury and settled into a bucolic and happy life with her new owner. Often she thought about how life had changed since she'd come to live with the girl she now knew to be called Emily. Willow had also learned that the boxes on wheels were called cars, the long boxes with many wheels were lorries and the motorway had a strange human name of M6.

***

Thinking about the day she left the field, the memory, like her nightmare played in her head. Cars and lorries were stationary, their eyes glaring as sirens wailed and blue lights flashed. Humans in bright yellow clothing had spent a long time trying to free her until a nice lady vet called Moira told her she had come to make her comfortable. Unfortunately, Mr Clifford the money-grabbing bastard had also arrived on the scene. "I look after this pony," he told Moira in an officious manner, "So if you don't mind stepping aside."

"I'm sorry but this pony now belongs to my client," she said tilting her head towards the man who stood on the hard shoulder hugging a sobbing girl. "So if you can step aside please."

"Do you think it has any broken bones?"

"I'll ascertain her condition as soon as I've made her more comfortable."

"I wouldn't waste my drugs on that old nag, just put it to sleep. I have a gun in my car." Willow let out a weak-sounding whinny and Moira turned and under her breath said to Mr Clifford, "Fuck off before I put a bullet into you, you moronic little shit."

Willow watched as Mr Neville and Miss Trudy managed to push their way through the hedge and climb over the fence that bordered the field. Pushing her face into a hole in the side of the horse box, Trudy clucked her tongue and told Willow she'd stay with her until she was safely off the motorway.

"Do you know this pony?" asked Moira.

"Yes, my boyfriend used to look after her. She's named Willow."

"Well Willow needs to remain calm, so can you continue talking to her, she seems to recognise your voice. I need to check her over." The lady vet turned to the pony and looking into her worried eyes she said, "Do you have any broken bones?" Willow responded by thinking; I can't tell you as I don't have a working knowledge of equine anatomy, because I'm a fucking pony.

***

Breakfast soon pushed the nightmare to the back of Willow's mind and as the sun warmed the paddock she strolled down to where Emily was sitting on the grass picking daisies. She nudged the small girl and her little hand reached up and stroked Willow's velvety nose. Willow wondered what Emily was doing and tilted her head questioningly.

"I'm making you a daisy chain necklace," Emily said, "because we have a splendid surprise for you this afternoon."

A surprise, thought Willow, how exciting. I wonder what it could be. She let Emily carry on picking and joining the white and yellow flowers and walked over to the fence to look over the lane, maybe the surprise was there.

Many hours passed but having no concept of time they meant nothing to the sand-coloured pony. She looked at the garland of daisies that Emily had made, they were hanging from the gatepost. If Copper was here, she'd have eaten them. Willow rarely thought about the other horses, to do so made her feel sad, even thinking about Roger the cantankerous donkey would make her eyes misty.

"Oh crap," she said under her breath, "Thinking about the others has now brought my mood down."

Her blue mood was lifted by curiosity as the sound of something mechanical coming up the lane took her attention. She cantered to the fence and saw a car pulling a box on wheels along the lane, behind it she saw another smaller car and she felt certain she recognised the people sitting inside it.

The vehicles stopped and Willow watched as out of the small car climbed Mr Neville, "Is this my surprise," she whinnied with excitement watching him open the gate and stand aside for the box on wheels to enter her paddock backwards.

Emily called her over, clucking her tongue and Willow trotted up to her and bent forward as the daisy chain was placed over her head.

Miss Trudy gave her a wave and held up a small pink human for her to see. "Hello darling," she called. "This is our baby and we've called her Willow."

So, that's my surprise Willow thought, a little pink human named after me.

"Here we go," Mr Neville said standing on one side of the box on wheels with Emily's father on the other. They opened the latches and dropped down the rear door and a familiar voice called out her name.

"Applejack," Willow shouted.

Mr Neville walked Applejack down the ramp and Miss Trudy called out, "The pantomime people heard Applejack inside the trailer and they rescued him before he was sent to Shanghai."

"But how did you get here?" Willow asked her friend.

"The humans said they didn't know how I had got inside the trailer. I heard one say that they needed to contact Mr Neville as I was last seen in his field."

"And they brought you back here?"

"Yes. Did you miss me?"

Willow didn't answer her friend, the lump in her throat made neighing impossible. Applejack rubbed his nose against hers.

"Look they're kissing," Emily shouted.

"No more dressing up?" Applejack asked.

"No. No more dressing up."

And while the humans drank lukewarm tea from a flask Miss Trudy had brought with her, the two horses chased each other around the paddock, rolled on the grass and knew that they were finally safe.

The End

Barry Lillie
New books for 2024

January	52 Weeks
April	Saving Springbrook
July	Under Italian Stars